# THE DEVIL'S OWN DEAR SON

*Books by James Branch Cabell*

## Biography of the Life of Manuel

BEYOND LIFE · FIGURES OF EARTH · THE SILVER STAL-
LION · THE WITCH-WOMAN · DOMNEI · CHIVALRY · JUR-
GEN · THE LINE OF LOVE · THE HIGH PLACE · GALLAN-
TRY · SOMETHING ABOUT EVE · THE CERTAIN HOUR · THE
CORDS OF VANITY · FROM THE HIDDEN WAY · THE JEWEL
MERCHANTS · THE RIVET IN GRANDFATHER'S NECK · THE
EAGLE'S SHADOW · THE CREAM OF THE JEST · THE LINE-
AGE OF LICHFIELD · STRAWS AND PRAYER-BOOKS · TOWN-
SEND OF LICHFIELD, SOME OF US, PREFACE TO THE PAST,
ETC.

## The Nightmare Has Triplets

SMIRT · SMITH · SMIRE

## Heirs and Assigns

HAMLET HAD AN UNCLE · THE KING WAS IN HIS COUNT-
ING HOUSE · THE FIRST GENTLEMAN OF AMERICA

## It Happened in Florida

THE ST. JOHNS (WITH A. J. HANNA) · THERE WERE TWO
PIRATES · THE DEVIL'S OWN DEAR SON

## Their Lives and Letters

THESE RESTLESS HEADS · SPECIAL DELIVERY · LADIES AND
GENTLEMEN · LET ME LIE

## Genealogies

BRANCHIANA · BRANCH OF ABINGDON · THE MAJORS AND
THEIR MARRIAGES

# THE DEVIL'S OWN DEAR SON

*A Comedy of the Fatted Calf*

JAMES BRANCH CABELL

*"And when he came to himself, he said . . .*
*I will arise and go to my father."*

*1949*

*Farrar, Straus and Company · New York*

MANUFACTURED IN THE U. S. A.
BY H. WOLFF, NEW YORK
DESIGNED BY STEFAN SALTER

# ✧§ TABLE OF CONTENTS §✧

*A Preface* ❧

# ABOUT THE BOOK'S BACKGROUND

———————————————

*"He said to his disciples, Make them sit down by fifties in a company. And they did so."*

—LUKE, IX, 14, 15

## ❦ ABOUT THE BOOK'S BACKGROUND ❧

THIS BOOK, which somewhat appallingly appears to be my fiftieth book, completes the trilogy called *It Happened in Florida;* and is, as one should perhaps explain, the same story which a while earlier was announced as being "in preparation" under the title *I Go to My Father.*

—For originally the tale was written in the first person, as an autobiography; and was then recast after the fact grew noticeable that, in middle life, Diego's opinions as to most of his own doings, and as to many of the events in which he had become involved, were biassed and almost wholly self-complacent. That frame of mind, in life's placid evening, is no doubt pardonable enough for a prospering and well-thought-of-citizen of what all oratory assures us to be the greatest country which the sun has ever shone upon. Yet I found it to be here and there a misleading frame of mind in which to narrate this special story; and I so abandoned my first outlines, lest you should think that I think Diego's conduct to have been flawless always.

I do not think this. I find some of his actions, in common with a number of Diego's beliefs, to be unpraiseworthy; and at any rate a few of both of them to partake of the incredible. Me it astounds, for an example, that anybody could speak of the tourist trade of Florida as being "self-concededly half deceptive."

By-and-by, so reflection tells me, I may be concocting a preface at large to this my final trilogy, which deals with a selected number of persons who, in the manner of gargoyles, have figured with a grotesque prominence in Florida's well-nigh uniformly fantastic chronicle. For the present I confine my tediousness to considering the locale of almost all this book, and of a main portion of the trilogy, which is the city of St. Augustine.

I first came to this city by accident and Florida State Highway Number One, in the January of 1935, so that I might die rather more comfortably from the after affects of pneumonia. And of the sedately green Plaza of St. Augustine, which at the instant was interpenetrated and gold-washed by the sunlight of a superb afternoon, I became enamoured, subconsciously, when I passed through it, upon the back seat of an automobile, at a time when I was very ill and half drugged and propped up among seven rather large pillows.

—For we were then upon our way to a Floridian city, somewhat farther south, which I found to be a flaunting and cheapjack and atrocious city. It followed that, without any least lack of fretfulness,

I voiced my potentially moribund wishes to go back to "that old-looking place where the men were playing cards in the park." Among these card players, so I discovered later, were both Captain José Gasparilla and Mr. B. B. Dodd.

At the time I did not know the name of this place. I knew only that I liked the appearance of it. And inasmuch as the whims of expiring persons ought to be gratified, we did go back rather promptly to "that old-looking place," which, after some little inquiry, we found out was called St. Augustine.

Abetted, and misled perhaps, by the not wholly unpublicized climate of Florida, I thereupon, in my desiderated city, so far neglected the ethics of medical science as to live through a type of pneumonia (I forget its exact number) which, at that period, no proper-minded patient was supposed to survive, as my physicians did not conceal from me. They were quite civil about it, I needs admit; but even so, it was with an air of expecting an apology.

Well, and here to abridge a tortuous long story which could not possibly interest anybody, ever since 1935, I have spent some part of each winter in St. Augustine, as a "winter resident"—at first through a mélange of accidents, which included the rashness of my recovery from two yet other attacks of pneumonia, and later because, in common with an invalid son and the unfortunate female who has to make up my mind for me, I liked St. Augustine, and the people of St. Augustine, and their manner of living.

This is not, I grant you, an emotion wholly proper to any Virginian as regards a city so lacking in good taste as to have been settled as far back as 1565, and always since then to have remained in the same place. Such tactlessness entails a great deal too much awkward explanation about the priority of Jamestown's settlement in 1607, as well as about the permanence of Jamestown; so that, as a body, we Virginians incline to feel that the less which is said about St. Augustine, the better.

Here I am heretic; and I confess as much with all suitable contrition.

Now what in particular I like about St. Augustine, a whit even above the tiny city's ancient and tranquil appearance, is its Utopian atmosphere of good-will. It is the only place known to me in which, as an affair of course, one speaks to, and in which one casually embarks upon long talks with, complete strangers.

In part, I suppose, this springs from St. Augustine's being almost wholly dependent upon its tourist trade. The townspeople thus have found it the rôle of common-sense to make themselves and their city agreeable to the tourists, upon whose patronage, alike, hinge the annual income of the townspeople and the civic welfare of St. Augustine at large. And the townspeople in this way have contracted, and they maintain, a perhaps professional but a highly pleasing habit of being affable to all and sundry. They adhere to this practice, so rumor tells me, in dealing with their own families, even with their own husbands.

Meanwhile the tourists are upon a vacation. They for the while are living—as my friend John Charteris once phrased to me this fine carefreedom —"in an atmosphere of holiday detachment from the ordinary duties and obligations of existence." So everybody has become genial; an epidemic prevails of the amiable; and under its influence even I, who in my time have been accredited with every sort of perversity except only that of being oversociable by nature, continue with a perplexed interest to observe myself discoursing en tête-à-tête with persons, whether male or female, whom I never saw before, and whose names remain unknown to me, as to our impressions of Florida, and our private affairs "back home," and whatsoever other matters may occur to each of us. We chat thus pleasantly for a while, with so large intimacy, upon one of the benches of St. Augustine, under a sub-tropical roofing either of palm trees or of live oaks; and we then part, upon the most cordial terms conceivable, not ever to meet again.

Now I like that. I enjoy finding in St. Augustine an all-pervading friendliness toward, and an apparently frank faith in, one's fellow creatures such as I do not find anywhere else.

Moreover, do I enjoy the compactness of St. Augustine. During almost four centuries the growth of this city has remained so negligible that even nowadays whenever you need to go anywhere in it, you have but to put on your hat and do so. There exist, it is true, outside what our realtors and poetic license term the Old Spanish Quarter, some sprawling suburbs in which dwell—here to be quoting from Diego's childish impressions—an unimportant number of such persons as work in stores or for the Florida East Coast Railway or upon the shrimp boats; and still other persons who are colored people. Yet into these nebulous and it well may be imperfectly civilized areas we winter residents of St. Augustine have no more call to be adventuring our elderly bodies, at curiosity's wild beck, than into Borneo or Texas or Sing Sing. We have heard from these suburbs no avocation.

So we winter residents do not ever have to depend upon an automobile or a bus or a streetcar to get us anywhere; and this slight-seeming circumstance, to my judgment, very much simplifies and sweetens existence, an always neighborly existence in which (excluding the tourists) every third or fourth person whom you encounter upon the street proves a daily acquaintance.

There, furthermore, is no possible "parking problem" when you enter afoot the business district to do your shopping (with the sales people all known to you), or to attend a play or a moving picture; nor in the better-thought-of residence district either, when you take part in this or the other staid festivity or pay a social visit. It is only the tourists who during their passage through St. Augustine do now and then have to confront that modern solicitude, the parking problem; and for whose special benefit the streets of thrifty-minded St. Augustine, throughout the last year or so, have been set abristle with parking meters.

The obligation faces me at this point to distinguish between a tourist and a winter resident.— For a winter resident is not merely, as the uninitiated might presume, a person who resides in St. Augustine throughout the winter, or even throughout several winters. Your true winter resident needs, in addition, upon his or her arrival in the city, to have been vouched for as a desirable acquaintance by someone among, in Diego's phrase, the people-you-know.

But the tourists, so nearly as I can put the affair, are persons who come to St. Augustine without any such specific credentials. Most of these tourists pause but for a day, or it may be for a couple of days, to gaze gapingly at the antiquities of the Nation's Oldest City; and then go somewhere else. Yet other tourists stop at one or another hotel for their two weeks' vacation, or perhaps they may stay on for a month or even longer; but during this period they consort with their own kind. Should they return for the following winter, they still remain tourists; nor, one should add, does it at all matter with what glories they may grace the pages of the *Social Register* or of *Who's Who in America*.

When tourists who are likewise celebrities of any such high nature appear among us, then the *St. Augustine Record* does ask for an interview about how very favorably these various famous persons have been impressed by the Narrow Streets, and by the Over-hanging Balconies, and by the Quaint Old-World Atmosphere, of the Nation's Oldest City. But beyond that bit of politeness nobody really notices their existence except only the employees of the stores, or of the souvenir shops, or of the hotels they patronize, and the efficient personable young woman who collects from them their admission

*xviii*

fees, including tax, to this or to the other antiquity of St. Augustine.

I do not mean that by us winter residents the tourists are treated as pariahs; but simply that a person who comes to St. Augustine unrecommended by any of the people-you-know stays always and forever a tourist. My point is merely that we winter residents, and in particular those of us who for a number of winters have been enhived at the same hotel in which the tourist has become a "paying guest," do not forgather with this alien. There is no snubbing involved, because, as I have told you, in St. Augustine everybody speaks genially to everybody else. It is but that we winter residents are clannish; that we have our own special interests; and that tourists are not among these interests.

We winter residents return to St. Augustine, and to our former quarters in St. Augustine, toward the middle of November as near as may be; and we remain until April. We are familiar one with another, and we are familiar also with the local aristocracy of St. Augustine, such as the Arredondos and the Zapos and, in some incommunicably lower degree, the Dodds.

I digress here to remark that I long ago gave up any attempt to understand just what does divide this aristocracy from the other year-round inhabitants of St. Augustine: for it is not birth exactly, and it has no concern with wealth (which indeed is considered somewhat vulgar, although pardonable here and there), nor with individual charm, nor with a person's being in any particular profession or in any special business, so far as ever I have been able to appraise this bland blind mystery. It is merely a division which exists; and which is recognized, accurately if tacitly, by all the persons upon each side of it.

But I was speaking, rather, of us winter residents. We come from all portions of North America, with a preponderance of New Englanders and with a notable infusion, nowadays, of Americans who had made their homes in Europe prior to the Second World War; and none of us is young. One notes among us a fair number of married couples and an occasional footloose male; but by long odds is the reputedly gentle sex the more frequent, for the most part in the form of stoutish widows with in-edited gray hair, who do not always refrain from anecdotes concerning the brilliance of their various grandchildren "back home."

Our favorite topic, though, is arthritis. We compare our symptoms, and we discuss the very latest infallible cure for this malady with a tolerant scepticism. Nor does "a heart condition" lack devotees. In each of these topics do a majority of us winter residents take, nowadays, an interest which is not all impersonal. And yet for some odd reason, never made plain to me, we consider it a social blunder to speak of dentures. Cancer we prefer not even to think about.

We winter residents, like Diego after his return to St. Augustine, have finished, *deo volente*, with the more strenuous passages of our living; we have given up, like him, those never so many unfulfilled aspirations which we nourished in youth; and there is really nothing of clamant interest to which we may now look forward, I suppose, upon this side of our death beds: but none the less, still like Diego, do we manage to get along in fair comfort for a limited while longer.

Yes, and the limits of this while are made continually the more vivid through the fact that every year some three or four of our small colony die. We then grieve for these far familiars; yet we grieve temperately. —For after all, this annual toll-taking has lost long ago any element of surprise. We expect it. We have become case-hardened to a calamity which is likewise a cliché.

And besides that, our tribe is increased every year by some three or four yet other persons fairly advanced toward the mortician's parlor, who have come among us properly vouched for; and thus, there is no collective difference left visual in our colony. So somewhat humdrumly indeed do the most of us winter residents of St. Augustine tend to resemble one another as go our general traits that common-sense may well question if, in reality, there has been made any change at all.

We who as yet survive among the winter residents, we at any rate, have learned how to accept each current year's necrology with an appropriate vocal regret; and then to get back, a mere wee trifle desperately perhaps, to our several diversions before, to us also, these demure junketings will have been forbidden forever.

—Because just as in St. Augustine Diego has his various social and religious connections to content his middle life, and Mr. B. B. Dodd his gin rummy and the Waverley Novels, even so do we winter residents contrive among ourselves in St. Augustine our staid diversions, unceasingly. We have our card playing, our theatre going, our moving pictures, the "at homes" to which we are bidden by the townspeople, our lending libraries, and our tea parties and our luncheon parties also, either at the Old Spanish Treasury Garden, facing on Quaint Old-World St. George Street, or in the Dolphin Restaurant near Marineland, or perhaps "at the shrimp place" upon Corbett's Wharf. By gaieties so multiform is not any day left un-asparkle.

Most of us, like Diego, are the members of a book

club which supplies us with three pounds of reading-matter every month. We are thus qualified, not littlely, to discuss the current novels and to revere the varied brilliancies of Francis X. Flubberdub and Gideon Gibberish, of Miss Natalie B. English and of Miss Laura C. Nugatory. We appraise with a chirping and benevolent interest these æsthetic phenomena, rather seriously.

Then too a fair or at any rate a female portion of us are members of the St. Augustine Arts Club; and such winter residents may be noted at all times in all parts of the Old Spanish Quarter commemorating, a mere shade rheumatically, either in oil or in water colors, some subdivision of real estate. To the public at large the results are by-and-by made free, in the pale pink headquarters of the St. Augustine Arts Club, facing upon Quaint Old-World Charlotte Street, along with tea and cakes and sandwiches, as well as at least one group of sea gulls in flight, a couple of paintings misrepresenting the St. Johns River, and never any less than eight still-life studies of recognizable flowers, arranged graciously in an unmistakable vase.

Nor is this by any means a complete summary of our cultural activities. Very many lecturers, in return for a small silver offering at the door, instruct us relentlessly as to topics of an improving nature. A select group of colored persons—not wholly, it has been suggested, in retaliation for having been denied their proper civil rights—pass from one hotel to another hotel, and sing "spirituals" to us, once or twice every winter. We elicit yet further mental stimulants from the pursuit of our foreign relief work, and from our church festivals, and from our Sunday evening musicales at the Ponce de León Hotel.

None of these employments is hilarious, no one of these amusements seems especially amusing. Yet the sum total of them allows to us aging but, as yet, not all-infirm persons no moment in which to become unoccupied or reflective upon the twilit futility of our latter-day existence. That a down-to-date precisian may right-mindedly label us frumps, I am not denying; that we are even those odd obsolescent creatures such as used to be called ladies and gentlemen, I concede with blushes: and I protest merely that we enjoy being thus reprehensible, just among ourselves, without injuring anyone else in particular, now that our prime has gone by, and our youth's brave foolish notions have been dismissed, like Diego's dream castle, with a partly amused shrug.

Such then, to my experience, is the "atmosphere" and the quiddity of St. Augustine, like that of a quiet island among the inconsequential and tumultuary and ever-changing streams of St. Augustine's tourist trade. Such is the aura of quite candidly exclusive, and perhaps snobbish, but stout-hearted frustration in which Diego was reared, and to which he returned, stout-heartedly.

Meanwhile we winter residents are not always so equitable in judgment as Diego became. —For, as I have granted, we tend to regard remotely, and with a frank touch of hauteur, "those tourists," when the latter bustle about St. Augustine so as to revere the antiquities of Their Nation's Oldest City, and then to go a-sightseeing somewhere else, after these strident nomads have left in St. Augustine a fair portion of the money which was put aside for the expense of their vacation.

Yet it is the tourists, rather than time-mellowed we or any of our time-mellowed friends among the local gentry, who support the time-mellowed city of St. Augustine. The antiquities which fetched these tourists toward the efficient, glassed-in young women who collect admission fees including tax, and these antiquities alone, have made possible for us winter residents our snug, placid domiciles between November and April; so that in a respectful emulation of Diego, we in clear justice ought to esteem the antiquities of St. Augustine as being among our assets and as our benefactors. We should look with admiration upon the Fountain of Youth,

and the Spot Near Which Ponce de León Landed,
and the Spanish Governors' Mansion, and the Oldest Wooden School House, and the Huguenot Cemetery, and all other kindred antiquities. Whensoever
we pass by any one of these antiquities, we in fact
ought to genuflect.

I am afraid that not many of us reason thus thoroughly and closely. We have not visited the antiquities of St. Augustine in never so long; and when we
speak of them we incline toward hypercriticism.

But I, at any rate, I am properly grateful to the
antiquities of St. Augustine. I regard them one and
all with an uncriticizing fondness. I do not think
that the question of their exact authenticity is important, inasmuch as, by and large, they compose
an exhibit which suitably impresses, and which
more than contents, tourists. It follows, I submit,
that after the admission fees, including tax, have
been paid, neither the proprietors of these antiquities nor the federal government—nor beyond doubt
the tourists—have any reason to complain; and the
entire transaction has become, to my finding, an
enterprise no whit less altruistic than it is patriotic
and profitable to commerce.

Once upon a time I had thought to complete a
book about that special group of us winter residents
who lived in the hotel of which Diego and his wife

took charge after this story had ended. But, as I began by saying, the present volume appears to be the fiftieth book, of this or the other size, and of varying natures, which I have published. —For I do not pause here to count those forty-odd revised versions upon which I have labored with an enjoyment very far more deep than many persons ever got out of them.

I instead pause to consider reverently my own genius for time-wasting, now that each final grouping of my so very many publications has been attended to; and to weigh likewise (do you let me add), with a respectfulness which is not any tinge less awe-stricken, the appealing and the appalling neatness of that fifty for a sum total.

"However—!" as Mrs. Catherine Mary Smith remarks hereinafter, concerning a rather more important topic. And upon the whole I agree with her.

*St. Augustine, Florida*
*27 November 1948*

*Part One* ❧

## HOW IT WAS IN THE BEGINNING

*"Though thy beginning was small, yet thy latter end should greatly increase. . . . Prepare thyself to the search."*

—JOB, VIII, 7, 8

# 1 ❧

Now, to begin with, when Diego de Arredondo Dodd became subject to time and chance, through the indiscretion of being born, that couple to whom a stork had delivered him were conducting a tourist home. Through a touch of that makeshift for humor which one takes to be as definitely an American product as are corn pudding and mental immaturity, this tourist home was called Bide-A-While; and it faced upon Matanzas Bay, at St. Augustine, which is in Florida.

So right in front of your house (as Diego was to remember these matters afterward) there was a wide and a sort of gray-colored road, called Bay Street, in between the four gray steps which people walked on when they came up into your yard and the gray low sea-wall, alongside which a row of gray-green palm trees lived despondently, on account of their being over-flooded so often with salt water. It made the palm trees look like big worn-out shaving brushes.

And the road which was right in front of your house went north to Fort Marion, and around the Fort Green, toward Jacksonville, where all of you went sometimes, so as to buy things. The stores were bigger in Jacksonville. But the other way, the road would take you to Ormond, where that rich Mr. John D. Rockefeller lived, and so to Daytona Beach, which was as far as you had ever been south.

If people kept on going south then the road went to still other places, where people could have lots of fun while they were being robbed of their money in almost no time at all. The way that people spent their money in those newfangled hotels and at the night clubs, in Miami and around Palm Beach, so your mother said, was just simply a sin and a shame; and there ought to be a law about it.

In a location thus favored by its circumstances, the Bide-A-While Tourist Home had many patrons (punctiliously termed "paying guests"), who stayed there for a night, or it might be they would stay for two nights if they wanted to look at the real antiquities as well as at the more liberally advertised imitation antiquities of the Oldest City in the United States. Almost every afternoon in the tourist season, along about sunset, either you or your father used to hang out upon the front door knob a sign which said, "Sorry No Vacancies."

But the Bide-A-While Tourist Home did not serve

meals, because your mother was born an Arredondo. An Arredondo could not be expected to wear herself out by slaving in the kitchen for a pack of riffraff who, if they wanted to, could get something to eat at a restaurant, or at either one of the drug stores. Moreover, that was why your father ought to be running the Pedro Menéndez de Avilés Guest House, with a coat of arms out in front of it, and some new paint on the house, instead of a tourist home, because a tourist home was tacky. But a guest house would have sounded all right for an Arredondo to be living in it.

—To which your father used to reply that the Arredondos were fine people, except for the way they got mixed up with magic-working and ghosts, and with familiar spirits too, Angelica, like your Aunt Isabel, such as a church member might just as well leave alone.

That, your mother would point out, did not have anything whatever, Mr. Dodd, to do with it.

Still, your father would say, the Bide-A-While Tourist Home had always been called the Bide-A-While Tourist Home, ever since Colonel Theodore Roosevelt and his Rough Riders had been over in Cuba because they remembered the *Maine*. And before that too. Anyhow, he stopped here himself one night and was more than pleasant to everybody. Not even you, Angelica, could be starting any argument about that.

Nobody wanted to, said your mother. Anybody with one single solitary ray of good sense knew very well that, by rights, Cuba had always belonged to Spain ever since whenever it was; and when the Arredondos were Spanish ladies and gentlemen, Mr. Dodd. But those Roosevelts were nothing except Dutchmen, no matter which way you looked at it, nor how long you kept on talking about them, when they did not have anything at all to do with a tourist home's being tacky.

And your father would say, "Yes, Angelica."

But if you started to call it after Menéndez, and a guest house too, then who in this world, your father would just simply want somebody to tell him, was going to pay for changing the signs on Florida State Highway Number One which said, "Let Your Next Stop Be at the Bide-A-While Tourist Home Sweet-Slumber Innerspring Mattresses and Locked Garages"? And besides that, when people married into a tourist home of their own free will and accord, Angelica, and always had a roof over their heads anyhow, along with a fair to average, steady income out of the tourist trade, you ought not to be finding fault all day long, and every day in the year, about everything you can think about.

Then your beautiful but high-spirited young

mother would begin to talk about skinflints and
people who were so pig-headed, Mr. Dodd, that
they could not see what was for their own good,
not even when you told them about it over and
over again, and when you put up with their not
giving you a sensible answer, instead of looking at
you in that lah-de-dah, high-and-mighty way, as if
you were a dog or something, and when it was all
just as plain as the nose on your face.

After that, your mild-eyed, gray-haired father
would fidget, sort of like a horse with a fly on it, in
his big green-covered chair, where he sat most of
his time; and your father would say,—

"Yes, Angelica."

Nor, Mr. Dodd (your mother would continue),
could anything very well be more plain than the
nose which every one of the Dodds had, exactly
like a flat little turned-up snout, and thank goodness, nobody who was named Arredondo had ever
thought about having such a nose.

And your father would tell her, "Methinks, said
the Archbishop of Tyre, that this controversy
might, without dishonor to any party, end at this
point."

That was something which your father said
came out of a fat book, colored like wet bricks,
called *The Betrothed* and *The Talisman*, by Sir
Walter Scott, Bart. Your father seemed to think

7

that what the Archbishop of Tyre had said was something ladies did not remember quite often enough. So your father was always telling your mother what the Archbishop of Tyre had said; and your mother said he was trying to be funny, and that she did not think he was at all funny.

She thought, instead, that you and your archbishops, Mr. Dodd, and your tacky tourist home, without even an oil circulator in it to take the chill off in the morning, so that those fault-finding, good-for-nothing tourists are always complaining about it so as to drive anybody half crazy, are enough, and if you want an honest opinion, Mr. Dodd, it is a great deal more than enough, to try the patience of a saint. And especially with all the other things that I have to put up with, too.

—To which your father would reply, "Yes, Angelica."

But he did not ever do anything about it. And so you and your father and your mother kept on living in the Bide-A-While Tourist Home.

## 2 ба

IN THIS manner did the childhood of Diego de Arredondo Dodd become familiar with that incomprehensible but remunerative race called tourists, who came to St. Augustine, and who spent money in St. Augustine, and then went away. You were polite to them, because they were paying guests. If they gave you ten cents or a quarter for telling them how to get to the Oldest House, or to Fort Marion, or to the City Gates, or to the Fountain of Youth, or even a whole dollar, sometimes, you said that certainly was nice of them. But you did not think that when they were at home they could amount to very much, or be like the Arredondos.

They were just tourists; and from the first of December until the first of April, upon the road which was right in front of your house, these tourists were always going through St. Augustine, either to the north or toward the south, in two large and ever-changing streams, as it were, of unimportant gay faces which you did not notice in particular.

It was only the drowsy, gray-and-green city of St. Augustine which did not change, except only so very slowly that you did not notice this changing either, or at least not among the people-you-knew; for so did your callow conservatism divide the native aristocracy of St. Augustine from such persons as worked in stores, or for the East Coast Railway, or upon the shrimp boats, or who lived in West Augustine, or who were colored people.

Now and then someone of the people-you-knew would die. There would be a half a column about

it upon the last page of the *St. Augustine Record;*
and your father and your mother would have to
decide whether just to leave cards and send a nice
bunch of gladiolus, or one of those wreaths which
cost as much as five dollars. And sometimes two of
the younger people-you-knew got married, so that
Miss So-and-so would have to be called Mrs. Some-
body-else and she would not be living in the same
house any longer, after your father and your
mother had sent her a nice cut-glass vase. Or perhaps your mother would simply be compelled, Mr.
Dodd, to pick out just a little something the next
time she went over to Jacksonville—and take it out
of the housekeeping money, she supposed—because
some yet other people-you-knew had got a red-col-
ored small baby, with hardly any hair at all; and
they were kin to the Arredondos.

But, by and large, the people-you-knew appeared
to stay pretty much as they had always been ever
since you could remember. And you believed that
the people-you-knew were a thrifty and progressive and well-conducted, big-hearted community,
such as were a credit to the Oldest City in the
United States and to its Quaint Old-World Atmosphere, because they all said so themselves. But they
were not especially exciting to live with.

And so when Diego de Arredondo Dodd had finished at the Ketterlinus High School, with a di-

ploma that had his name on it, and had started to shave almost every day, and to read the front page of the *St. Augustine Record,* where the out-of-town news was, then you began to wonder about those very much more exciting-sounding places beyond Jacksonville and beyond Daytona Beach which the tourists went to, all the time between December and April, upon the road which was right in front of your house.

"These places do not concern us," said your father, who was called Mr. Bartholomew Burton Dodd, "except that when the tourists go to these places they almost always stop over in St. Augustine to look at the Narrow Streets and the Overhanging Balconies of the Oldest City in the United States. And when they do that it is good for the tourist trade."

"Yes, but—" you said, just as all young persons have always needed to say when they considered the axioms of their elders.

"And besides that, as I was telling you," your father went on, in the slow way that he usually talked, "in a lot of these places, Diego, people are up to all sorts of things. But here we have a roof over our heads at any rate, and we have a fair to average business, and we have a small steady income out of the tourist trade."

"Yes, but, sir—" you replied, yet again, because

in those days you did not think at all highly of a small steady income. You meant, instead, to have just oodles of money.

"Do you keep the tourist home, and the tourist home will keep you, Diego," said your father.

"And for goodness' sake do you marry that Catherine Mary of yours," said your mother, "and get settled down as soon as may be, because she will make you a good enough sort of wife as these modern girls go, for flappers they may well call them. —Which is not saying much, what with their turkey-trotting and their bunny-hugging and hardly any skirts at all. But she will keep you in order better than most of them, if"—your mother added, with pessimism—"anybody can."

"Well, may be I will let Catherine Mary marry me some day or another," you agreed generously, "because I like her right much more than the other girls. And I suppose I will have to settle down and run the Bide-A-While Tourist Home, by-and-by. But there are some other things which I have got to do first."

"And what are these things, Diego?" your father asked.

"Well, sir, before I get married and settle down, and before I have had the place repainted and put in an oil circulator, I want to become very rich, like Mr. John D. Rockefeller, and very famous—

like Rudolph Valentino, I mean, and Mr. Jimmy Walker and the Prince of Wales. And in short, sir, I intend to see something of the world at large."

"You will be far better off here, Diego," said your father, and now he was talking real slow, even for him, "with a small steady income out of the tourist trade."

"Nevertheless, sir, I have need to be going to and fro in the earth, and to be walking up and down in it."

You knew what you meant. But you wondered why you were saying it in that way. You just had to, somehow.

Then your father looked at your mother for a grave, quiet while before he said anything more. The clock upon the mantelpiece ticked. Your father was not at all surprised, you noticed, but just sort of sad about something or other; and when he spoke he said what did not sound like him, or even seem to make much sense. Your father said,—

"The boy has fire in him."

"And is that my fault, Mr. Dodd?" your mother asked, indignantly. "Only of course in this house everything is my fault!"

"It is a point as to which I am not starting any argument, Angelica, because I was over in Jacksonville at the funeral."

"Yes, and a fine uncle he turned out to be," said

your mother, "with every penny that he had in the world going to charity after we had been sending him a necktie or some handkerchiefs every Christmas, and upon his birthday too, as regular as clockwork, for more than five years. But that," your mother concluded, with the resignation of a married woman to whom the depravity of human nature has been made familiar in her home circle, "that is you Dodds, all over."

Your father answered, "So I am simply saying, Angelica, that if your Diego de Arredondo Dodd has made up his mind to see something of the world at large, and to be going to and fro in the earth, and to be walking up and down in it, like one of his relatives, why, then you had better be fixing some lunch for him to take along with him."

"But I never heard of such nonsense," said your mother, "at his age, Mr. Dodd, nor did anybody else either."

"And you know that as well as I do, Angelica," your father continued, without paying one least bit of attention to what your mother had said about nonsense, "because I am not starting any argument as to whether you know it much better. I mean, about letting Diego go his own way; but not of course without any lunch."

Then your mother said that even so, Mr. Dodd, she did wish the poor boy did not have fire in him.

Your father replied that if wishes were horses, then most of us would ride to the devil. That was another one of the things which he said right often. And your beautiful young mother twisted her hands together, and her lower lip got to shaking, but for this once she did not start to arguing about what your father had said.

She only wondered if you had better take the green stone along with you? And your father told her, no, not by any means, because anybody who had fire in him would be getting into quite enough trouble without it.

Everything which the two of them said sounded sort of mixed up, but you did not worry about this, now that your parents were allowing you to become very rich and very famous, and to see something of the world at large.

## 3 ঽ

THE NEXT THING which Diego de Arredondo Dodd did was to talk with Catherine Mary Zapo. She was dear to you; she was your girl friend; and to the young eyes with which you regarded a world ensured against any more wars by the League of Nations, and exhilarated by the homemade gin of Prohibition, and restored to eternal normalcy by the Republican Party, young Catherine Mary Zapo appeared wholly lovely.

Catherine Mary was very much too nice and too good-looking, you assured her, to have to live in a tourist home, and be bothered with riffraff who fussed about there not being enough heat in the morning, when your father was going to put in an oil circulator just as soon as he could possibly afford it, and who were too lazy to go out for their breakfast. She really ought, you explained yet furthermore, to be an empress or a queen of somewhere or another, or may be the wife of the President of the United States.

But Catherine Mary said that Mr. Coolidge was married already; and that she would rather marry you, anyhow. So you told her may be you would let her be Mrs. Diego de Arredondo Dodd by-and-by.

Catherine Mary said, "You stuck-up thing, you!" and she slapped you upon your cheek, but she did not hit you very hard.

After that, you and Catherine Mary kissed each other again. And you and Catherine Mary decided that when you came back from having seen the world at large, along with your riches and your famousness, then you would pull down the Bide-A-While Tourist Home, after you had bought all the land behind it as far back as to Charlotte Street; and that you would build in its place a castle, facing upon Bay Street, for you and Catherine Mary to live in.

Nor was this going to be any ordinary sort of castle. Inside, of course, it would be fixed up pretty much like the Ponce de León Hotel, where the rich tourists stayed who did not have to think about money, because they had a great deal more money than was good for them, so your mother said, only everything would be much handsomer. But the outside of this castle was going to be like the sunset which you and Catherine Mary were looking at right then.

You and Catherine Mary were looking at it from the Fort Green, just a little bit of way outside the City Gates of St. Augustine that they have a picture of on the post cards and in all the guide books. You and Catherine Mary were sitting upon a green bench underneath a twisted-up big cedar tree. The winds which come over Matanzas Bay from out of the Atlantic Ocean had pushed at this tree so hard and for such a long time that it had done almost all its growing on the south-west side of itself. There was right much Spanish moss hanging down from this tree, like Santa Claus beards; and in the sunset they were shiny like silver.

Anyhow, you and Catherine Mary were sitting

17

underneath this cedar tree, and were holding each other's hands because you were going away; and both of you were looking at what you told Catherine Mary was a real curious sort of sunset.

Catherine Mary said she was too unhappy to be bothering about sunsets, but that even so, she would always remember this one, because it was just too adorable.

That sunset had pearl-colored walls in it, and pale blue walls, and somebody had hung over the side of these walls a lot of bright banners, in the way that people used to do in King Arthur's times in your book called the *Mabinogion*. You could see that beyond these walls there was a castle which had towers with gold tops to them; and every one of these towers was red, like the towers at the Ponce de León Hotel, except that the red was a very great deal redder and more shiny-looking.

It was a big castle; there was some kind of magic in this castle; and altogether it was just the sort of castle which Diego de Arredondo Dodd and Catherine Mary Zapo ought to be living in, you felt, as the two of you sat there hand in hand upon the Fort Green, and you approved of the magnificence of your future home, immediately beyond the dark live oaks and the palm trees and the magnolia trees and the gray and brown tombstones of the Huguenot Cemetery.

And both of you two children were lucky enough, so did you reflect afterward, in that neither one of you could foresee anything which was going to happen, a while later on, in this very same Huguenot Cemetery.

*Part Two* ❧

# WHAT VARIED DUTIES REQUIRED

*"They kept also the feast of tabernacles . . . according to the custom, as the duty of every day required."*

—EZRA, III, 4

## 4 ૨☙

So was it, in the way about which I have told you, that with youth's high heart to incite him, and with youth's arrogance to mislead him, the fine-looking, all-ignorant youngster, whose adventurous body Diego de Arredondo Dodd inhabited once upon a time, went away from his native, and small, and remuneratively quaint city, to take his tribute of the world.

When Diego came back again, his mother had been dead for nine years and three months. His father was white-haired and more contented-looking. Catherine Mary had found time to marry, and to get a divorce also, after this Mr. Smith of Branlon had deserted her; and the city of St. Augustine had been changed variously by the dictates of its professional Quaint Old-World Atmosphere.

During Diego's absence, the Bridge of Lions had been constructed across Matanzas Bay, so that those tourists who preferred to travel along the Coastal Highway and the Ocean Boulevard would be induced to pass through St. Augustine whether they wanted to or not; and would spend some of their money in the Nation's Oldest City. All other requirements of a tourist were now being attended to by an impressive Spanish Mission Style Recreational Center and Tourist Club—conveniently adjoining an Ancient Cemetery—as well as by a number of brand-new Old Spanish Souvenir Shops and Old Spanish Over-hanging Balconies and Old Spanish Homes and Old Spanish Water Wheels and Old Spanish Inns. All these additions to the Oldest City in the United States were, noncommittally, Said to Have Been Erected at a Period Prior to 1763.

Moreover, the Spot Near Which Ponce de León Landed in 1513 had been moved down the seacoast from its undesirable former position, which was at least twenty miles away from anywhere else, into the Plaza of St. Augustine, so that, without having to leave the National Highway, all tourists could look at the exact spot where the history of their country began, and at a statue of Ponce de León also, with a befitting reverence and some natural wonder as to the shortness of his body from the waist up.

The Spanish Governors' Mansion, As Completed in 1603, had been demolished and rebuilded throughout, upon a rather more hidalgo-like scale of magnificence, over and above having been made the St. Augustine post office. In the most convenient tract of city property available, where the tourists would have an abundance of parking space, a Prehistoric Timucuan Indian Burial Ground had been established, brimful of exposed skeletons in what Diego considered to be a somewhat imaginatively immaculate state of preservation. And Fort Marion he found to be labeled, nowadays, The Historic Castillo de San Marcos, As Builded by the Spaniards in the Years Following 1672, with an Admission Fee of Only Twelve Cents Including Tax.

In short, the Oldest City in the United States had been so lavishly replenished with antiquities that the tourist trade now prospered as never before in all the highly colored, long history of St. Augustine.

A number of the people-you-knew had died during Diego's absence, but those of them who survived received him with a complaisant friendliness, because, upon his mother's side, Diego ranked as one of the Arredondos. Moreover, with that money which Diego had inherited from old Aubrey Thompson's going into bankruptcy, and from Jack Chantrey's lack of plain common-sense precautions in a dark alley, and from poor Roger Maldahyde's having shot himself in Diego's apartments, Diego established a reputable banking account. Diego purchased some Government Bonds and such other securities as the imaginativeness of stock brokers elects to call gilt-edged; and Diego assisted his father, loquaciously but with competence, to manage the Bide-A-While Tourist Home.

Diego de Arredondo Dodd, in fine, was well thought of everywhere. He joined the Kiwanis Club, and the Chamber of Commerce, and the Hotel Men's Association, and the Business and Professional Men's Association, and the Benevolent and Protective Order of Elks (Lodge 829, in which he figured as Esteemed Leading Knight), and the Humane Society, and the St. Augustine Historical Society and Institute of Science, as well as a number of still other confraternities of which I forget the names. I recall, however, that he was neither a Mason nor an Odd Fellow.

He was elected to the vestry of his church. He was made treasurer of the Laymen's League. And the possibility of his becoming one of the five members of the City Commission was discussed nowadays with a gratifying frequency.

Among the winter residents of St. Augustine, Diego was in high request as a fourth at bridge; for his game was considered sound, even though, said the meticulous, it was marred now and then by a tendency to talk too much during critical moments. Diego attended most of the weekly card parties, as well as the weekly teas, at the various hotels of St. Augustine. Not often was Diego absent from a Sunday evening musicale at the Ponce de

León. And the junior Mr. Dodd was to be seen discoursing, affably and with a superior instructiveness, as to composition and modernity and "mere colored photographs" at almost every exhibit of the St. Augustine Arts Club.

Diego, in the interests of culture, likewise subscribed for a couple of seats, in the third row, at each opening Friday night of the Artillery Lane Players; and in one of these seats you, as a rule, observed Mrs. Catherine M. Smith, who had passed that afternoon, it was evident, at her hairdresser's. Both of these coincidences evoked shrugs, which were wholly friendly, among the winter residents and the people-you-knew.

Moreover, Diego's views upon modern literature were esteemed by the more serious-minded of St. Augustine's inhabitants, with whom he was accustomed to discuss, in a vein of befitting gravity, the very latest publications of Francis X. Flubberdub and of Gideon Gibberish, of Natalie B. English and of Laura C. Nugatory, and of yet other pre-eminent American writers. For Diego nowadays was a member of two book clubs which appealed to the better instincts of every member of one's family, and which supplied him every month with a book weighing not less than three pounds, at a reduction from the publishers' price.

Diego, in short, liked being listened to. Yet since

no one of the people-you-knew had bothered to ask Diego about his travels, he did not ever talk about his travels, or about his adventuring into any strange foreign parts where the winter residents and the tourists lived when they were at home— not even with Catherine Mary. She knew what men were, said Catherine Mary, in tones which discouraged any such talking.

## 5 &

DIEGO found that Catherine Mary, nowadays, appeared unobtrusively but firmly certain as to her complete knowledge about everything—except only, of course, such matters as, in Catherine Mary's phrase, people would be a great deal better off if they left alone.

She was brisk, and yet, too, she was quiet. She exhaled invincibility. She, as it were, faced life with an alert air of being ready to dispose of, immediately but without turmoil, any such circumstances as might be foolhardy enough to let Mrs. Catherine M. Smith cope with them. In brief, the schooling of time and her excursus, or, as Diego put it, her round trip, into matrimony had made of the Catherine Mary whom in Diego's youth he had adored inarticulately a person of whom Diego, at bottom, was a little afraid.

Even so, he remained in love with her. Or rather, to phrase the affair with somewhat more exactness, he delighted in the all-comprehensive and kind-hearted efficiency of Catherine Mary, and in the dear, simple goodness of her—as well as, let it be confessed, in the ability of Diego de Arredondo Dodd, just now and then, to make this handsome and self-complacent and domineering person feel that, without noticing it, she had said something which sounded rather disconnected and muddled.

This does not mean that Catherine Mary ever bothered about Diego's being so smart-alecky that, as she explained, somebody really ought to smack him good and hard. Catherine Mary at least knew what she meant. With a complete precision Mrs. Catherine M. Smith knew how she intended to settle any matter whatsoever about which she was talking. And she knew also that any other settlement of it would not be worth considering.

So when Diego started to be smart-alecky, then she would color up slightly; and that was all. Catherine Mary stayed unperturbed by, as she put it, Diego's perpetual nonsense.

She said only that some people were always trying to be funny; and that she did not think they were at all funny.

Diego replied that it was immodest of her to be talking to him as if he were her husband.

Such people, in their own way, Catherine Mary now mentioned aloofly, might have more intelligence than she had ever pretended to have, or at any rate more book sense, but it was along with very little politeness, if you wanted an honest opinion.

"But I never said—" Diego began.

"You did not have to say it," Catherine Mary stated, conclusively, "when you were looking at me just as if I were a dog or something."

Diego sighed at this point. He then answered that whenever he looked at a dog it was with affection, because he was fond of dogs; and that for this reason he had not looked at Catherine Mary as if she were a dog, or even as if she were something.

"But you could not see the way in which you were looking at me, Diego; and I could," Catherine Mary pointed out.

Afterward, she began to cry. It followed that, with some slight apprehensiveness, Diego kissed this normally so authoritative and rather large but still handsome housewife.

Then Catherine Mary became suitably indignant. She said that really of all things!

"Nevertheless," said Diego, "you liked it. You are as pleased as Punch, or perhaps the proper gender is Judy, now that I have surrendered to your strategic blandishments."

Catherine Mary said that she did not know what in the world Diego was talking about; that not for one single solitary moment was she going to put up with any such conduct; and that she had thought he had more respect for her.

"You said that the first time," Diego observed critically.

"Why, but of course I did," Catherine Mary answered; and in her wide, bright, very pale blue eyes now showed a quiet wonder as to Diego's obtuseness. "A girl has to, when she has been properly brought up and does not intend to have just anybody taking liberties with her. And so do I, for that matter, so long as you men stay what you are."

Diego said, politely, "Do you permit me then, my dearest, to allay your fawnlike trepidations by saying that I have surrendered with the wholly honorable intention of making you an unsatisfactory husband."

That almost every one of them did was Catherine Mary's cryptic answer; and besides, she thought that at our time of life, Diego, we ought to be extremely careful about doing anything which we might come to regret afterwards.

Diego, at that, reared back expansively. He tucked his right thumb into his right armpit, and his left thumb into his left armpit; and in this, his very frequent posture, nowadays, he spoke affably, with his chin well lifted. Diego, in brief, was now being what Catherine Mary was so inappreciative of as to call Mr. Biggety Big.

"I do not know about you, Mrs. Catherine M. Smith," Diego stated, "nor just how many skeletons may lurk in your clothes closets and pantry and comfort stations—"

"You hush up!" said Catherine Mary.

"But nobody who married me," Diego continued, "has ever lived to repent of it afterwards, if only upon account of the pains which until this afternoon I have taken to remain a bachelor. And when it comes to prattling about 'our time of life,' I need to remind you, my life's one love, that I have but lately entered my thirties."

"You will be forty-one years old next July, Mr. Biggety Big, and I am already thirty-nine, as you know perfectly well, so that you are not talking good sense."

Diego removed his thumbs from his armpits. He did not quite like being called Mr. Biggety Big, because he knew that just now and then it was justifiable. But his voice remained instructive.

"To the contrary," Diego pointed out, "I am speaking pearls of wisdom; because after all, when you come to look at it from the standpoint of intelligence and of vital statistics, what do a mere meager eight or nine years amount to? I mean, of course, so long as through taking proper precautions to avoid any form of self-indulgence such as might make life enjoyable, almost anybody can live to be eighty."

That, Catherine Mary said, was only some more of Diego's nonsense; but even so, she added with a continuance in resignation, the Bide-A-While Tourist Home needed a woman to keep the servants in hand. You ought to have got rid of that Maria Dolores years ago, what with her breaking simply everything she touched, and just sweeping the dust under the rugs. Men did not know what servants were.

—Which, Diego admitted, was true, so far as it went, as well as being a handsome tribute to the purity of the male mind.

Catherine Mary told him to stop talking as if he did not have one single solitary grain of good sense.

"—For, Diego de Arredondo Dodd, you know you are talking nonsense. Everybody in St. Augustine remembers how we used to be engaged, or at any rate almost, anyhow, because of course we were nothing but children. And I am not denying," Catherine Mary continued, fair-mindedly, "that engaged persons are expected to get married."

"So it was out of your deference to public opinion

33

that you got married, Mrs. Catherine M. Smith?"

"And would it have been proper for me to show no more self-respect than to be sitting around and waiting for a young man that had left me so that he could go wandering about goodness only knows where?"

"Yet as I remember it, you fickle-hearted and misbehaving gill-flirt, he left you just temporarily and with large bucketfuls of tears. He left you in order that by-and-by, and in fact within two shakes of a lamb's tail, he might be fetching back, along with his famousness, enough million dollar notes to be building up for you a fine, gay castle made out of the higher grade clouds of sunset. And that castle was to snare the eye of its every beholder with beauty, and inflame his heart into enviousness, precisely where, as some part of me regrets to observe even nowadays, my dear, the Bide-A-While Tourist Home stands unaltered."

Catherine Mary replied with a little wistfulness; and yet, too, she was now speaking with that majestic air of omniscience which Diego knew to be droll, but in point of fact found intimidating. She said, with the patience of one who is explaining the obvious to the feeble-minded:

"It was not for any Catherine Mary Smith that castle was to be builded, Diego, but for a nitwit girl who talked with a good-for-nothing, bragging, book-reading young rapscallion, over yonder outside the City Gates, upon the Fort Green, more years before last year than it would be polite to remember. And she was to live in that castle with a boy who went away from St. Augustine and did not ever come back. But for you and me, Diego, now that we are getting on, the tourist home will serve well enough. Because it is just as Mr. Dodd says——"

"I know, my dear. Keep the tourist home, and the tourist home will keep you. And in fact, if only we can ever get around to putting in an oil circulator, and having the place repainted, I believe it will, rather comfortably. Nevertheless, I think it is well to remember that the two of us once owned a castle in the sunset, and that we saw our castle quite plainly, even though we did not ever enter it."

Catherine Mary touched the back of Diego's hand in a gesture which he found to be partly compassionate and wholly proprietorial.

"It is only young people, you very silly, forever talking Diego de Arredondo Dodd, who can see that castle; and my eyes are not what they used to be."

"They are quiet eyes, dear Catherine Mary. They do not ask any questions. There is no doubt in them, not even about me, but only a bright, tranquil self-confidence. Your eyes, in brief, rather frighten your lifelong adorer. They predict **a** highly henpecked future. So by all means, let us get married," said Diego, resignedly, "since you made up your mind about it the first day I came back to St. Augustine."

"How did you know?" said Catherine Mary.

She then colored up slightly. She said that never in her entire life had she seen so much self-conceit as some people seemed to have, though goodness only knew why.

"However—!" Diego's betrothed wife added, ominously. "And as for that Maria Dolores—!" she said also, in the tone of a person who looks forward to combining a duty with a pleasure.

## 6 ໃ◌

A WHILE LATER in the same day—which happened to be the thirtieth of April, when the tourist season was at an end—Diego told his father about how, after Diego had pleaded with her for a long time, Catherine Mary Smith had consented to let Diego become her second husband; and about how she was going to be a great help to both of them in conducting the Bide-A-While Tourist Home.

One does not know how to describe the half-sympathetic and the half-troubled way in which

*36*

Mr. Bartholomew Burton Dodd then looked at Diego, beyond saying that it showed Mr. Dodd was a widower.

"She will lay down the law for you, Diego," said Mr. Dodd. "She will not let you call your soul your own, not for one single minute, Diego; and so far as that goes, it may be good for you."

"I regret, sir, that you should think my soul requires a special custodian."

"To the best of my experience, Diego, when you get married you have to choose between having that or else a continual argument," Mr. Dodd philosophized.

He then placed a pink slip of paper in *Ivanhoe,* to show where he had left off reading. He laid aside the book.

"—And," said Mr. Dodd, with tolerance, "I have always believed in people's getting married, or at any rate moderately. But the trouble is that, the very next thing you know, you two may be having a baby."

"Well, sir, and as we scholars put it, *Et tu, Brute!* for so did you have a baby."

Here was a point as to which Mr. Dodd appeared open-minded.

"That, in a manner of speaking, is true, Diego; and ever since you got over being a baby, I have found you to be satisfactory enough when you were not talking. For you are so far like your mother that you do stop talking sometimes. But," Mr. Dodd observed, with the large calm of one whom circumstances have compelled to restate a truism, "that does not prove what sort of baby you might be having."

"I do not think I could well settle that, sir"—and Diego coughed discreetly—"except by the usual methods."

"—And if," Mr. Dodd explained, mildly, "if it had horns or a tail, or even all three of them, Diego, you would not like that."

"To be wholly honest with you, sir, I would not. They would be, I think, to almost any nursery an unwelcome addition."

"Nor would the Zapos like it either, Diego, because they are universally respected as being one of our very oldest families."

"I admit the possibility of the Zapos' not rejoicing over horns and a tail upon, as it were, their hearthstone," Diego replied, with candor as well as with curiosity. "Only, just what are we talking about?"

Mr. Dodd was aggrieved.

"I was telling you, Diego, how they came over from Minorca, some time back in the 1700's. And of course your mother and I did not talk very much about it. Or was it from Greece, now? Because you

38

know how people are, Diego, when it comes to exaggerating anything which seems out of the ordinary, quite apart from the Arredondos having been mixed up in more than enough of that sort of thing already, if you ask me. So we decided not to discuss it with anybody; and I still think we were right."

"Not for one instant, sir, would I question you were right. Your complete rightness reflects complete credit upon you, I may even make bold to say, in the light of my as yet limited information—"

"At any rate, that was the way it seemed to us at the time, Diego; and in fact, now I think of it, I believe the Zapos came over as far back as with the Turnbull Colony. And it was Turnbull's wife, of course, instead of the Zapos, who came from Greece. That was what I had in mind, Diego."

"I can follow your train of thought," Diego replied, "so far as goes its freightage with the Turnbull Colony and with the Zapos' origin. Only, what was it, sir, that you were completely right about?"

"Why, but I was telling you about you, Diego. Because we had been married for a good while and did not have any children. So you did come rather as a surprise, what with my having to go over to Jacksonville to my uncle's funeral, and his not leaving us anything after all, and what with the tour-

ist season's being over, so that there was not anybody whatever in the house."

"Yet the laws of nature are no less Medic than
Persian," Diego answered; "and because of this
trait, sir, well, but, so to speak, biology leads me
to infer that my mother may have been somewhere
in the neighborhood, even if I did come rather as a
surprise."

"But of course, Diego, your mother was here.
Somebody had to be, just in case; and after all, he
was not her uncle. He was my uncle. So you ought
not to keep on changing the subject when I am
trying to tell you how the cook had gone home the
very first minute after she finished with supper and
had washed up the dishes. They all do nowadays,
without consulting your convenience one way or
the other."

"Still, sir, inasmuch as we were not talking
about cooks—"

"But we were, Diego; because that left your
mother all alone by the fireplace when the wind
was blowing a great deal. She almost thought a
thunder storm was coming up. I mean the one in
the back parlor, not the fireplace upstairs. You see,
Diego, she had not yet gone upstairs, because it
was still quite early in the evening, and in fact, the
cook had hardly got out of the house."

"Yes, sir, no doubt she had; but even in the light

of that circumstance, I do not wholly comprehend, no, not as yet, sir, what happened."

"Her name was Matilda Clare," Diego's father continued, reminiscently, "and she was trifling, of course, like all the rest of them. But she was beyond doubt the best fish cook I ever saw anywhere. So as I was telling you, a gust of wind came down the chimney, and then flames spread all over the hearth. They were even outside the fender. She went north to a restaurant, I believe, just before you get to Philadelphia somewhere. And it was a near thing that your mother's skirts did not take fire. But she was spared to us for that while at any rate. So it might have been worse, Diego, because the ladies used to wear very long skirts at that time."

"And was that all, sir?"

Diego's father looked over the top of his spectacles with an air of some slight surprise.

"Why, but of course, Diego. She was not even scorched."

"Nevertheless, sir, I do not understand what this fine fish cook had to do with my coming rather as a surprise, nor why my mother should have been having an open fire in the summer time, nor how, if you were in Jacksonville overnight—"

"But, Diego, that was on account of my uncle's funeral. Besides, it was for two nights. And nobody would ever be having a fire in the middle of July, without my having to remind you about your own birthday's coming on the sixteenth."

"Still, sir, you did say something as to flames——"

"I told you quite plainly," Mr. Dodd informed Diego, "that the flames came down the chimney, a great wave of flames. Only, you like to talk so much that you never listen to anybody."

"But where did they come from, sir?"

"How would I know?" Mr. Dodd inquired, reasonably. "I tell you, though, it was a near thing, what with her being all alone in the house, and me a good forty miles away in the funeral parlor. She might very well have been burned to death like the girl over on West King Street, at the grocer's. At any rate, that is where you came from."

"I do not see, sir, how I could have come from the grocer's. Not even at the larger chain stores where you put everything in a wire baby carriage do they keep any babies on sale. Nor do I see what I had to do with the girl at the grocer's——"

"And who could see that, Diego, when you were away on your travels at the time? Besides, nobody ever said that you did, so far as I can remember, or that there was any man in it at all, but only the hot water heater's being out of order. They are a great convenience of course, but you have to watch them. The girl was entirely respectable."

"Well, then, sir," Diego asked, yet again, and without losing his patience, because he had known his father now for some forty years, "whatever is it that we are talking about?"

"Why, but I was simply telling you, Diego, how the fire went back up the chimney, and how it left you upon the hearth, stark naked and squealing and holding a queer little green stone in your hand. In fact, it is still over yonder, just behind you, in the cupboard."

"Oh, but come now, sir—!" said Diego, with what, there is no denying, was a blending of the incredulous with his surprise.

"So you had to have your milk and some diapers," said the placid, dunderheaded old gentleman who but now had disclaimed being Diego's father. "Then, what with one thing and another, and our not having had any children, your mother decided to keep you. And whatever was I to do about it without starting an argument?"

Here was a question so completely academic that Diego dismissed it in silence. He and Mr. Dodd both knew that Mr. Dodd's so pretty young wife, and Diego's putative mother, had been born an Arredondo, with an unreticent appreciation of this fact, as well as of the social status and the mentality of mere Dodds.

Nevertheless, in this story as to Diego's apparently supernatural origin, Diego submitted aloud, as he reared back and tucked his thumbs into his armpits, the sceptic might, it seemed just possible, sir, detect a flavor of the improbable.

But with this notion his foster father (as precision compels one to call Mr. Dodd henceforward) dissented. Nor was there any least bit of sense, Mr. Dodd added, in anybody's swelling up like a toad frog and starting to use long words, the way that some people liked to do, because ever since that very same Don Diego de Arredondo whose name had come down to Diego took to concerning himself with matters which a church member ought to have left alone, although to be sure they were Roman Catholics in those days, there had been more or less of that sort of thing in the family. You came to expect it by-and-by after, as you might put it, you had married into it; and nobody ought to be saying that what was usual was the least bit improbable.

"Even so, sir——" Diego began, impressively but quite ineffectively.

——For they both knew, said Mr. Dodd, and so did a great many other people right here in town, how that very same Don Diego de Arredondo, and not anybody else, had got rid of Captain José Gasparilla and had set up his shadow as a pirate over yonder upon the West Coast, where, in Mr. Dodd's opinion, the tourists might find a better train connection but nothing like so good a climate as in St. Augustine.

"Nevertheless, sir—" said Diego.

There had been no doubt whatever, Mr. Dodd continued tranquilly, about that business of Diego's Cousin Lucas de Arredondo and the wax image, a sort of pink-colored wax; and in fact, if he had not been on the City Commission the police might have been in it too. But the Mayor had seen about that. The way in which Diego's Uncle Manuel de Arredondo had behaved with the ghost of a Spanish governor's wife was an out-and-out scandal which people still talked about—although, to be sure, if it had not been that, it would have been something else, so Mr. Dodd supposed, because that was how people were. At any rate, Diego's Aunt Isabel de Arredondo was getting toward an age when a self-respecting old lady would have stopped having a familiar spirit in and out of her bedroom long ago.

"Sir, if you will in any wise permit me to put in a word edgewise—" said Diego.

—Even if in the daytime it did look like a cat, said Mr. Dodd. But it looked quite different in the middle of the night, all the neighbors complained, and much later for that matter, nor did an ordinary cat talk what seemed to be Spanish at the top of a sort of squeaky little voice. So Diego's Aunt Isabel de Arredondo was still up to nobody could say what, no farther away than at her home over on St. George Street, as Diego knew perfectly well without trying to start any argument about it.

"Yes, but—" said Diego.

—Exactly like your mother, Mr. Dodd continued. Moreover, here was the green stone— which he now took out of the corner cupboard. And besides that, Mr. Dodd repeated with finality, he had not been anywhere near the fireplace on this particular night; so that nobody could expect him to remember what happened there.

Mr. Dodd then stated that a sane married man does not try to believe everything which his wife tells him, or to start an argument about any of it, either; and that wherever Diego might have come from, he was now at the Bide-A-While Tourist Home.

"So do you keep the tourist home, Diego, and the tourist home will keep you," was, in fine, the placid verdict which Bartholomew Burton Dodd evoked from all these matters.

"There is something in that, sir," Diego admitted; "and even under the immediate, first, and deplorably unsettling shock of discovering myself to be a changeling, I do not wish to contemn common-sense."

"In that case, Diego, the affair is settled; and methinks, said the Archbishop of Tyre, that this con-

*46*

troversy might, without dishonor to any party, end at this point. For now you can see for yourself what I meant about your getting married and having a baby, because it might take after, why, but goodness only knows who. The Zapos simply would not put up with it, Diego, nor would the vestry either."

"Yes, sir," said Diego, a little forlornly, "or at least, I mean, no, sir."

Still, Diego was not really uneasy about there being any diabolic additions to his not impossible baby, because he knew the four babies in the creating of whom he had collaborated during his travels had none of them possessed horns or a tail, but instead had been uncommonly fine-looking children. Diego did not feel at liberty, however, to take up this point with his foster father now that Diego had repented properly, a good while ago, about every one of these babies. For a middle-aged person who belonged to the best civic and social organizations to be talking about any such matters would not have sounded at all well.

Diego recollected, though, that each one of his illegitimate children, unaccountably, had been born red-headed; and that in each case the child's mother and Diego likewise, not here to mention her husband, had been surprised and more or less upset by this odd occurrence.

7 ᘓ

So was it that Diego first heard about what he
thought to be his unlikely origin; and Diego approved of the consideration with which his foster
father gave to Diego the same account of it which
Mr. Dodd's wife, more or less tactfully, had ren-
dered to Mr. Dodd. It was not possible perhaps for
Mr. Dodd, and most certainly not for Diego, quite
to believe this account; but good-breeding prompted
them, who were both Southern gentlemen, to pretend to believe it rather than to asperse the veracity
of a Southern gentlewoman whose memory they
revered.

Diego wished only that he could accept the affair
as calmly as did Mr. Dodd. An unhuman progen-
itor, it appeared obvious, had added Diego to Mr.
Dodd's household; and common-sense told Mr.
Dodd, as it told Diego also, that nothing whatever
could be gained by discussing an affair in which
common-sense was no more deeply involved than
in the Bible, so Diego reflected. Diego inclined
therefore to applaud his plump, white-haired foster
father's decision to accept without ostentation, or
any vain boasting, the compliment which an immortal personage, who traveled incognito, had be-
stowed upon the Bide-A-While Tourist Home by
staying there for an overnight visit to the Oldest

*48*

City in the United States; but Diego did not share in Mr. Dodd's equanimity.

And Diego began to envy this Bartholomew Burton Dodd, with whom Diego had lived for so long a while in close physical intimacy, but about whom Diego did not really know anything.

Bartholomew Burton Dodd adhered to his reasonably remunerative and slightly shabby tourist home—which still lacked, notably, an oil circulator, so as to take the chill off in the morning— because when people called it an ordinary, he had inherited this tourist home from his father, who had inherited it from his own father, and so on backward, even into the remote 1820's when President Monroe, a little while before this doubly patriotic Virginian allowed John Quincy Adams to write the Monroe Doctrine, had first violated it by swindling Spain out of Florida.

Bartholomew Burton Dodd held to the ways of his forefathers, who, to the extent of his knowledge about them, had always been, as he phrased it, "in the tourist trade," and who for a century and a quarter had got out of the tourist trade a small steady income.

Meanwhile the old gentleman was perhaps the most leisured person in all St. Augustine—which is a city, as Diego once put the matter, wherein haste has no home.

Throughout every morning Mr. Dodd read the *Florida Times-Union*. He sat meanwhile in his large green-covered chair, which had a rectangle of white lace pinned over each thickly padded arm and a square piece of white lace pinned high up to the back of it for a head rest. Mr. Dodd thus enacted the rôle of "looking after things" while tart-tongued, bronze-colored Maria Dolores Jackson—who now for seven years had condescended just to stay on for the rest of her month, and who after that was not going to keep on slaving for anybody—was "turning out" and "airing" the rooms, and changing the bed linen, of the Bide-A-While Tourist Home.

Then after lunch, upon clear afternoons, Mr. Dodd played rummy, or gin rummy—between which two games there was a subtle difference unknown to Diego, who had never played either one of them, but had heard rumors as to wild deuces being involved somehow—or at times Mr. Dodd played checkers, in the Plaza of St. Augustine. At five o'clock in the afternoon Mr. Dodd read the *St. Augustine Record*. And after supper Mr. Dodd talked with such tourists as might be his paying guests overnight, or else he read onward, for about two chapters farther, in whichever one of the Waverley Novels he happened during the current month to have under placid consideration.

For it was Mr. Dodd's custom to proceed unhurriedly through the romances of Sir Walter Scott according to their order in the twelve stout terra-cotta-colored volumes of Mr. Dodd's "library set," which contained two novels to each volume; and when he had finished *Anne of Geierstein*, then to begin all over again with *Waverley*. From his canon he excluded *Count Robert of Paris* and *Castle Dangerous* and, somewhat oddly, *Redgauntlet;* otherwise he omitted nothing. Since he read slowly, the Waverley Novels and the *Florida Times-Union* and the *St. Augustine Record* supplied his literary needs.

Nor did Mr. Dodd appear to have any other needs which being in the tourist trade left unsatiated. You kept on meeting, as Mr. Dodd liked to point out, all sorts of people, Diego, from just simply everywhere, while they were having a vacation, and were not worrying about anything. —Not even, Mr. Dodd would add, about our overhead charges, which we have to consider, of course, or else go straight into bankruptcy, or about having to pay a little bit more for their gasoline and their liquor and their cigarettes, and for pretty much everything else too, so they tell me, on account of our state taxes and our city taxes.

Diego replied sedately that, in point of fact, sir, when it came to the tourist trade, the gorges of

Colorado were far less gorgeous than the gouges of Florida, which provide us Dodds with daily bread as well as an occasional slice of cake.

—So they did not worry you, either, Mr. Dodd continued tranquilly, and without bothering to reprove Diego's nonsense. They just liked to sit around and talk about how things were back at home. It was a lot better than traveling yourself. It was real instructive.

Now Diego, in private, thought that Bartholomew Burton Dodd provided at least four-fifths of each and every conversation in which Mr. Dodd might be engaged, inasmuch as there was not any known, or even any conceivable, method of checking the old gentleman's calm discursiveness; yet Diego did not argue this point. He instead accepted the peculiarities of Bartholomew Burton Dodd fondly; and now in fact he inclined to envy the ways of Mr. Dodd, which begot a so placid incuriousness.

For Mr. Dodd did not waste his time in thinking about any such abstruse and unimportant matter as was that perhaps regrettable tendency to become involved in unearthly dealings which seemed common to the Arredondo family. If you married into it, of course, why, then there you were! Still, you did not have to be starting any argument about it.

This matter of Diego's birth did not concern any

of your daily vital interests, such as your two newspapers, or rummy and gin rummy, or the Waverley Novels, nor the tourist trade either; or at least,
it did not concern but just one supernatural tourist,
more than forty years back; and in consequence,
this matter—when you came to look at it quite
sensibly, and what with poor Angelica's being
dead, anyhow—did not really concern Bartholomew Burton Dodd.

Mr. Dodd, in brief, so Diego reflected, agreed
with the peace-preserving policy of the Archbishop
of Tyre in *The Talisman*; and had decided long
and long ago,—

"Methinks that this controversy might, without
dishonor to any party, end at this point."

But Diego was not like Mr. Dodd. Nor could
Diego hold to the ways of his forefathers as con-
tentedly as Mr. Dodd did, if only because the nature of Diego's forefathers was unknown to him;
and had become indeed the provoker of some un-
avoidably gloomy apprehensions.

## 8 ࿐

As a result of the mental biliousness which now
pervaded Diego's thoughts, he put on a white shirt
and his second-best dark blue suit along with a
black bow tie, such as Catherine Mary had told him

to wear in the evening without any vest, whenever Diego went out calling, because it made Diego seem almost exactly as if he had on a Tuxedo; and was very distinguished-looking.

After that, Diego went over to the home of the aged gentlewoman whom he had been reared to think about as his Great-Aunt Isabel de Arredondo; for every one of the people-you-knew accredited her with being a witch and a past mistress in all branches of infernal practices. Such sinister knowledge, Diego reflected, howsoever deplorable in the public utterances of any person whom middle-age and a small steady income had blessed with correct principles, might well be of use to him in private; and one does not like to be wasteful.

So Diego told Miss Arredondo all about everything. Or at any rate, Diego told her the same story which his foster father had told him; and Miss Isabel de Arredondo nodded over what Diego thought to be his well-nigh incredible narrative with a ruminative benevolence and no token of surprise.

She instead went on nodding, abstractedly, and with the air of a person who has made up her mind, under the pressure of resignation, it might have been, but once and for all, as to the world's imperfect nature.

And you thought about how very large was Aunt

Isabel. And how shapeless also. She was shaped like a helping to ice cream in uncommonly warm weather. Yet her face was stately; it made you think about, well, no particular Roman empress, but all those Roman empresses whose associates had to combine politeness with any personal safety; and above her boldly outlined features loomed an impressive structure of white hair, which was tinged with blue. Her clear brown eyes appeared always to be looking, with a flavor of amusement, at something a little way behind you.

She was not really Miss Arredondo, because she had been married four times; and, after divorcing her husbands one by one, had resumed with composure, after each divorce, her official status as a spinster. All her husbands had died long ago. It must have been a relief to them, upon the whole, or the divorce at any rate, because while Aunt Isabel was wholly good-humored about it, still she looked into and beyond you all the time.

Such were Diego's meditations in the while that he narrated his story, and the enormous, handsome old lady, whose age had become incredible and legendary a fair number of years before Diego was born, stayed attentive to him with an unsurprised amenity.

Then, at long last, Miss Arredondo spoke, in the most matter-of-fact fashion conceivable.

"It was probably Samaël the Seducer," she decided, "although of course it may have been any one of the seventy-two princes except Satan. His notions of morality are rather strict, the poor dear. They all see to it, Diego, that their children by mortal women are born in the manner you describe, because it is so much more convenient to the mother than is the repulsive and painful process of childbearing when the father is human."

"But, really, Aunt Isabel," said Diego, "or at least, ma'am, if you are still my Aunt Isabel—"

"Of our relationship, my dear, I am now doubly certain," Miss Arredondo replied; and she went on stroking the large, brown-and-white cat, called Rory, which lay in her lap, and which people said was her familiar spirit. "Yes, it might have been any one of them," she continued; "but Red Samaël is the only prince who has remained forever youthful; and so he has by long odds the most affectionate nature."

"Nevertheless, ma'am—" said Diego, inadequately.

"And Angelica combined with her amusing and agreeable conversation," Miss Arredondo added, "a shortness of temper which led the poor child into continual squabbles with every one of her acquaintances. But at bottom her heart was kindly. For it was her heart, Diego, you may depend upon it, which induced her, as a refined and compassionate female, to abridge and perhaps to omit an event or two which preceded your birth. For her to have been blurting out the complete story would have been painful to her husband. So she acted as befitted a considerate wife; and her conduct was praiseworthy."

"But whatever is it, Aunt Isabel, that you would imply?"

"My dear," Miss Arredondo returned, with a calm and condescending dignity, "I must entreat you to remember that I am a gentlewoman of the old school; and in my day, for a gentlewoman, after she was once married happily to the gentleman of her choice, not to have made equally happy a lover or two would have exposed her to a large deal of unfavorable comment. It would have appeared parsimonious; and people would have said she was setting up to become an eccentric. I admit that for Angelica to have selected an infernal spirit as, we must charitably hope, only one of her lovers was somewhat out of the ordinary, nowadays."

Here was a notion before which Diego recoiled with a suitable expression of horror, because, while he had been turning over in his mind this notion, it did not sound at all well when you put it into words.

"I cannot listen to such imputations," Diego stated stiffly.

"In fact," his Aunt Isabel continued, "with the exception of one or two of my earlier flirtations when I was an unthinking girl—and such a bouncing, fine piece of gaiety as I was in those days, my dear! —I cannot recall but four similar instances among the Arredondos whom I have known. In each case the child was relinquished to the father's keeping so as to avoid scandal. For you know how people do gossip about unaccounted-for babies, without being as broad-minded about the little dears as Bartholomew Dodd. There may of course" —Aunt Isabel added, conscientiously—"have been some still earlier instances. I can speak only as to my own time. Yet I am getting on in life nowadays."

"You speak, ma'am, with an excess of modesty," Diego protested. "For enough decades to confound arithmetic, in common with all human probability, you have been the marvel of Florida and a vital tribute to the supremacy of our average weather conditions and our mean daily temperature such as the entire tourist trade appreciates; and before which a discredited California gnashes its dentures. Nevertheless, not even from your revered lips—"

But again the gentle-voiced old lady interrupted

Diego; and now she smiled in the same instant that Miss Arredondo sighed reflectively.

"I permit them to say what they like, my dear, because I too have a kind heart. So I am willing to give everybody pleasure, by letting the newspapers and the chambers of commerce print articles about me and the Sunshine State and the Second Spanish Occupation and the Gulf Stream. But I bargained for my long life, Diego; and with whom I bargained need not matter to the inquisitive busybodies such as, alas, one has to encounter nowadays even in reputedly genteel circles."

"In fact, ma'am, in society, just as everywhere else, it is the scum which rises to the top."

"So when my time has run out," Miss Arredondo continued, "they will be finding me with my neck twisted and my body blasted; but it will have been a contented time, my dear, because a little depravity helps one on through life very smoothly. And in the place to which I am going afterward we Arredondos are well known, and our doings here upon earth are well thought of by the seventy-two princes, so that I shall be making shift to get on pleasantly enough, let us hope, in my decreed home."

"I have not the least doubt, Aunt Isabel," Diego said, politely, "that in any imaginable surroundings you will be universally respected and ad-

59

mired after you have quitted St. Augustine—and to everybody's regret, ma'am, I am certain—in favor of, well, as our rector prefers to call it, the place of departed spirits."

Miss Arredondo then inclined her bluish-tinted white head, in an acknowledgment of her nephew's courtesy. But she said only,—

"And now do you let me have a sight of that green stone, my dear, about which you were talking."

Diego gave it to her. His Aunt Isabel put on her reading glasses, which had large round tortoise-shell rims and caused her to resemble an owl. She looked at the carved small stone for some while.

The cat which was in her lap turned about so as to look at this stone. The cat lifted its right forepaw so as to touch the stone. The cat mewed.

"Why, but of course, Rory," said nidnodding Miss Arredondo, in the soft, dignified manner which was peculiar to her. She then added,—

"And so it has come back!"

"Do you mean, ma'am," Diego inquired, "that you recognize my, so to speak, birthstone?"

"I mean," the old lady answered, "that either this same stone or else a stone exactly like it used to belong to my own father. You will not easily conjecture the emotion with which I regard it. For my own father, my dear, during the proud days of what the narrow-minded termed his iniquity, was accustomed to wear just such a stone as his watch-fob. It is one among the many other qualities of this stone, so Rory tells me, that it makes the time whatever one may prefer to have it. And the stone came to him from his half-brother, although of course I do not refer to Rory's half-brother."

"Yes, ma'am, I quite understand you," said Diego, very affably, because in point of fact he did not.

"He had first received it, so I have always heard," Aunt Isabel continued, "as a personal gift from Samaël the Seducer. With that amiable personage my Uncle Antonio, or so they tell me at least, because a refined female does not like to seem boastful as to her own family, had the honor to be closely allied. One cannot deny that, as the genteel phrase it with a well-bred turn of speech such as nowadays, my dear, has become deplorably rare, their alliance was upon the wrong side of the blanket. Even so, it existed; and in consequence of it my Uncle Antonio, in addition to being a military engineer of distinction and a statesman who displayed fine gifts in the way of duplicity, also became one of Spain's leading sorcerers."

"But really, Aunt Isabel, do you think that to be repeating any such old ancient gossip can make for the true good of anybody concerned, or that it sounds quite respectable?"

Miss Arredondo then told Diego, with a dignified upbraiding in her handsome, shrewd face:

"Your own past doings, Diego de Arredondo Dodd, it may be, are not wholly that which your fellow Elks and your fellow Kiwanians and your fellow members of the Chamber of Commerce would be praising with orations. Nor perhaps," Miss Arredondo added, benignly, "would your fellow vestrymen be setting up every one of your doings as a model for the Young People's Service League."

At that, Diego's thumbs went into his armpits, and Diego reared back with somewhat the expansiveness of an amiable turkey gobbler.

"Now, but, Aunt Isabel, you know, I am certain, upon account of your wide experience and your civilized attitude toward the more deplorable aspects of human life in general, if I may speak thus frankly, because I am sure that no living bishop regrets them more deeply than I do, that when an inexperienced boy is trying to see something of the world at large, so very many things do happen—"

"Especially in bedrooms," Miss Arredondo suggested, still nidnodding.

"Well, sometimes perhaps, Aunt Isabel, inasmuch as I have found most up-to-date circles to consist largely of triangles. But what I really meant, ma'am, was just here and there. One then has very often to act, as it were, upon the spur of the moment and between the horns of a dilemma. In a position so delicate I do not pretend to be infallible. However, I am not egotistic, either. For which reasons, ma'am, I must venture to remind you it was not about me we were speaking, nor about any such sad slips as are natural enough in an inexperienced boy, but about my birthstone."

"Yes, and I was trying to tell you, Diego, when you started to talk your roundabout, long-winded, Chamber of Commerce, vestryman humbug, that I never saw it until this evening. But over and yet over again I have heard of a queer green stone which resembled this stone, from my most dear and honored stepfather, great José Gasparilla, the King of Pirates; and about how my own father, that same Diego de Arredondo whose name you bear, made use of this stone in what candor leads me to describe as a not wholly straightforward fashion."

"In fact, Aunt Isabel, a good while before that Cabell man who stays at the Buckingham had added new glories to St. Augustine by editing the memoirs of José Gasparilla, in the book called *There Were Two Pirates*," Diego remarked, reverently, "I likewise had heard, from my dear mother's lips, the old story as to how your stepfather was decoyed into the land without shadows, and how he spent nine years there."

"It seems only yesterday that the King of Pirates came swaggering down Artillery Lane, and that I first talked with him in our patio before breakfast," Diego's Aunt Isabel declared. "Dear me, but how it all comes back! I was barely eight at the time; but I was not too young, not even then, Diego, to get on amenably with a fine-looking, fine-talking practitioner of what, in this world of hypocrites, a refined female needs to call wickedness."

Thus speaking, smilingly, the old lady relapsed into a soft brief reverie such as Diego lacked the heart to disturb. You had to step lightly, he reflected, when you were trying to get around Aunt Isabel.

"So he married my mother about a month after that," Miss Arredondo resumed, by-and-by; "and I was Papa José's favorite among all his stepchildren. Over and yet over again, Diego, my dear Papa José has told me about this queer green stone shaped like a beetle, with this hole running through it, and about how it caused him to give up the profession of piracy, along with his shadow, and to become an ornament to the leading social circles of Florida."

Diego stayed silent, as he had learned how to do

occasionally when it appeared remunerative, in a whirl of doubts and of some unease.

Now the cat clawed at Miss Arredondo's left arm and mewed with insistence.

The old lady put aside the rose-tinged memories of her childhood, and she began to speak in a louder and more cheerful tone.

"As always, Rory gives good advice," she observed, affectionately, stroking the cat's mottled back, with a plump and a surprisingly small hand. "This most happy discovery very much brightens your prospects in the way of immunity from all forms of discontent; for I know how the stone is used. Your proper course, my dear, under the obligations of filial piety, as well as of your own self-interest, has become plain. You have but to approach your infernal father—and with a suitable amount of deference, as I need hardly mention to you, Diego, who so becomingly delight in humbug. No matter which one of the seventy-two princes of Hell your father may turn out to be, he will then give you whatever you may desire. They always do, the affectionate poor dears, without talking any cruel celestial nonsense about an eye for an eye and a tooth for a tooth."

Diego answered her calmly enough; and yet he spoke with a sudden elation of spirit.

"That is excellent hearing, Aunt Isabel. You see,

ma'am, I have enjoyed living, by and large, and I have found this world a fine residence, on account of my having tried always to be charitable and broad-minded about everybody's actions, including my own. Yet never in my life have I attained to what I most desired."

"You have only to ask for it now, my dear, even though in all likelihood you will not like it afterward. You gentlemen never do, I think, after having married four of what we ladies used to call our swains."

"Yes, but, Aunt Isabel, I do not know how to reach, well, let us say, the place of departed spirits, because it really does sound rather better than Hell, and inasmuch as our own rector, you must let me remind you again, prefers that expression when we are reciting the Apostles' Creed. I mean, so long as I stay alive. And even after I am dead, it seems highly improbable that a member of every one of the leading civic and social organizations of the Oldest City in the United States would not be ascending into Heaven a good while before the mortician had finished with making him look peaceful and dignified, and as natural as ever."

"That is as it may be," Aunt Isabel returned, with a considering sidelong glance such as Diego did not, upon the whole, regard as a complete compliment. But he smiled back at her affably now that the old lady's lifelong wickedness was about to come in so very usefully.

With a resumption of her customary benevolence, Miss Arredondo then told him what he must do in order to attain damnation; Diego listened with eager respect; and Diego said that he at once would conform with his revered aunt's how far more than inestimable advice.

"—Only," Diego submitted, in a high-minded and a purely experimental fashion, "I must first, of course, tell Catherine Mary about what filial piety, as it were, now demands of me."

"If you do," said Aunt Isabel, with decision, "your Catherine Mary will simply put her foot down. For these virtuous women, my dear, have their own strange notions, along with their own ways and means, about which I am thankful to say I know nothing. Catherine Mary will not ever let you go to Hell, should you permit her to have a finger in this piety."

"Yes, but, ma'am, since it is merely for a brief visit—"

And to such nonsense Aunt Isabel replied, from a point somewhere between compassion and exasperation:

"You must comprehend, Diego, that the Woman's Auxiliary of our church, and much more the Colonial Dames of America in the State of Florida, would disapprove of your going to Hell. And Catherine Mary, like me, is a member of both."

Then Diego admitted, nobly, "In fact, Aunt Isabel, so great is my affection for Catherine Mary, and so whole-hearted is my regard for her social position, that, just as you say, perhaps—"

"There is not ever any perhaps," Miss Arredondo stated, "after that pale-eyed, pig-headed Catherine Mary of yours has once put her foot down. You know that quite as well as I do. So, if you tell her, that will be the end of your correct filial obligations —you long-winded, rather lovable glib fraud!—as well as of your getting whatever you may desire."

Diego answered: "In fact, Aunt Isabel, just as you say, and as I was going on to observe, I do, no doubt, owe it to Catherine Mary's being on the Board of Governors, as I believe the Dames call it, and the St. Monica's Chapter also, as well as the Woman's Exchange—and to her peace of mind, too, because one ought not ever to be selfish and inconsiderate—to explain about anything which I intend to do after I have already done it. That will prevent any argument, ma'am, such as Catherine Mary might find distasteful."

Behind her reading glasses the magnified brown eyes of Miss Arredondo twinkled.

"For the present, my dear, perhaps it may. And after Catherine Mary has once married you, Diego, there will not ever be any argument in or about your household," Miss Arredondo assured him, speaking with a touch of commiseration.

"You mean, ma'am, that I shall have to put up with the obedience which a capable wife promises to and extorts from her husband? Well, I am not saying you are wrong; and it may be good for me, by and large. Meanwhile I stay, at any rate temporarily, a bachelor; and my filial obligations remain, so to speak, paramount."

## 9 ੭~

Now after Diego had uttered these correct sentiments with firmness, he kissed the left cheek of his Aunt Isabel with affection. He went northward from her home; he crossed the deserted Plaza; and he strolled up narrow St. George Street, under a medley of Old Spanish Over-hanging Balconies, toward the City Gates of St. Augustine, now that midnight was approaching.

Beneath the neon sign of an Old Spanish Eating House—a sign which at this late hour was unilluminated, but of which, with a pallid gray-blue gleaming, the plump convex lettering still offered to any and all tourists, Worlds Best Fried Shrimp, for there was no apostrophe in the "Worlds" of this sign—Diego then performed, almost flawlessly, the odd and pre-historic, yet simple, ceremony about which his Aunt Isabel had told him. Not until toward the conclusion of this ceremony did Diego fall into any positive error.

This means that, after his shadow had detached itself from his person, and Diego had folded it up into an inconspicuous thin parcel, Diego was about to hide it underneath the 8 Inch Howitzer Gun, Armament of Fort Marion, which stands to the right of the City Gates, when he was taken aback to observe that the projecting rim around the butt of this cannon was numbered xiii.

Now Diego was not at all superstitious, except about walking under ladders, or putting on his left-foot sock first, or laying any other book on top of a Bible. Yet it seemed unwise for Diego, at the start of his journey, thus to be wooing ill-luck through any over-daring, and in fact hubristic, alliance with the number thirteen.

What followed was that Diego crossed the street so as to put his folded-up shadow underneath the other small cannon, how far less ominously numbered xv, which stands to the left of the City Gates; and not until a good while afterward did Diego find out about his mistake. His eyes had deceived Diego when he read—in the moonlight, it must be recalled—the number of the first cannon. It in reality is marked xiiii. This slip, however, seems pardonable; almost anyone might have fallen into it; and it was the sole blunder which Diego de Arredondo Dodd committed during his first attempt at magic working.

After that, Diego passed through the City Gates of St. Augustine, upon the thirtieth of April, at midnight precisely, taking along with him the queer green stone. And now to the left hand of Diego, in a clear twilight with no shadows in it, a twilight such as by ordinary proclaims the beginning of dawn, showed that nineteenth-century burial ground which furthers the Quaint Old-World Atmosphere of the Nation's Oldest City by being called the Huguenot Cemetery.

Diego looked toward this burial ground with some interest. In fact, as the part owner of a tourist home, he knew that the Huguenot Cemetery was one of his assets.

"And the minor circumstance that no Huguenot has been buried there," Diego used to say, "we who are in the tourist trade are compelled by logic to dismiss as being irrelevant. We reflect that, after all, if only this grim mortuary relic of antiquity were in mere point of fact antique, and if ever any Huguenots had inhabited St. Augustine, a fair quota of them, quite conceivably at least, might have been buried in this cemetery. We then perceive that their so incredible negligence, even as to their own obsequies, ought not to be allowed to interfere with our income; and the Huguenot Cemetery stays a predominant Point of Interest in every one of our guide books. Q.," Diego would add, with a broad-minded and backward-rearing expansiveness, "E. D., as we scholars like to put it."

—Which was perhaps a digression. But our loquacious Diego did not object to a digression except when somebody else made it, just as I am doing here.

I had meant merely to record that Diego now looked toward this burial ground with some interest because, the nearer that he came to the Huguenot Cemetery, the more ghosts did he observe to be abroad among its tombs. And from this fact he deduced that the green stone which he now carried with him, in the small inside coat pocket of his second-best dark blue suit, had begun to exercise unusual qualities.

*Part Three*

# OF THE DEAD AND THE DAMNED ALSO

*"A dream cometh through the multitude of business;
and a fool's voice is known by multitude of words."*

—ECCLESIASTES, V, 3

## 10 &

WELL, and as I was telling you, Diego de Arredondo Dodd could see a rather large number of ghosts prowling about in the Huguenot Cemetery (upon account of this cemetery's gray walls' not being any higher than his navel), now that he carried in his pocket the queer green stone.

Yet with a mind centered upon his own concerns, Diego went by the place without noticing any of these dreadful visitants in particular. At this hour of the night their restiveness seemed natural enough. And in fact, without giving the matter a second thought, he would have ignored their vacation from the eternal homes to which divine justice had consigned them, if one of these ghosts had not chosen to glide through the cemetery wall, just as Diego so very often had seen a ghost do in moving pictures.

It approached Diego when he was crossing San Marco Avenue, immediately between the two traffic lights.

Since Diego knew that a ghost cannot speak until after the person who is being haunted has addressed it, he was thus forced, by the dictates of that courtesy which stays an ever-important requisite for people who are engaged in the tourist trade, and who have to humor the tourists, to inquire what this apparition needed.

The surprise of Diego was extreme when the creature responded, wailingly,—

"You ought to know right well what I have come for, you damn murdering Dago!"

Even then, however, it was not until after Diego had looked at the phantom rather more closely that he recognized Herbert Darnell, because this Mr. Darnell, who during his lifetime used to be pudgy and red-faced, was now of a pallid blue-gray color —resembling that of an extinguished neon sign, Diego reflected—and he was vaporous like smoke.

Well, and to be meeting Herbert Darnell again, there was no denying, seemed a little awkward. Yet Diego spoke civilly enough to the intrusive, somewhat tactless reprobate who had come out of Diego's put-by past, because Diego knew that at worst he could always outtalk Herbert Darnell.

So Diego suggested, first of all, that they step over to the sidewalk upon the north side of Orange Street, rather than stand here in the middle of the state highway, where a car might come by from any one of three directions. He carried, he explained, no accident insurance. It was one of those matters, Diego added, which you kept meaning to attend to, but just somehow did not ever get around to, like returning a lawn-mower or having the dentist check up on you.

And Diego continued in his attempt to reassure this ghost as to the fact of Diego's not harboring any rancor, by saying,—

"You must permit me to tell you, Herbert, with a candor which true friendship always justifies, that I have very often regretted the circumstances of your death."

The ghost answered, after having groaned hollowly, in accord with tradition,—

"You damn well ought to!"

"Even so," Diego resumed, "I was young at the period of your decease. I acted upon the impulse of a moment during which, as I must recall to your sense of justice, you did not leave me time for ample reflection. Nobody can expect an inexperienced boy—and especially when his entire future, so to speak, hangs in the balance—to exhibit complete self-control. So that it really does seem better, as people say, for us both to let bygones be bygones, even though, when you stop to think about it, Herbert, I do not see how a bygone could ever be anything else."

"You skunk!" Darnell replied, in a harsh tone of voice which Diego could not but deplore, as being uncivil, "and is this what you call remorse?"

"Come now," Diego said, "but again I must plead inexperience. It is not as if I were accustomed to being haunted; and in consequence I do not know how you would like me to be remorseful about what."

"You ought to be remorseful forever and forever about having took my life—" Darnell began, with a continuing evidence of that violent temper which, in common with syntax, the poor fellow was not able always to control.

"Why, but," Diego returned, patiently, "if that be your special grievance against me, you very certainly must know that I have not the power to restore you to the perils and anxieties of mortal life."

"Stop talking guff, you slimy, slick male puppy of a feminine dog!" was the tenor of the ghost's reply.

"And besides," said Diego, "you would now be too old to get much iniquity out of life. That is a point which, I submit to your calmer judgment, ought to be considered. You already had stomach ulcers, remember; you were nearing sixty; your blood pressure was high; your doctors had ordered you to give up smoking and alcohol in any form;

whereas I would hesitate to embarrass you by repeating what your wife used to tell me, but only in strict confidence of course, as to your lessened amative powers. So if you were still alive, Herbert, it would be in a penitentiary perhaps, on account of that banking transaction in Chicago, where you were so injudicious as to leave fingerprints, or at best you would be doddering about, nowadays, in a rolling chair. It follows that you are not really missing any one of the vicious delights which you used to get out of living."

"But," Darnell said, stubbornly, "you bumped me off."

"Well, waiving the King's English—and although merely to a certain extent, Herbert—that is true. And if it be your wish to awaken in me repentance for having committed that technical misdemeanor, the aspiration, while it is not based upon any really sound logic, might still, in its own limited way, be viewed as pardonable. It at worst would show a continued personal interest in my welfare. For this reason I would condone any such wish."

"Stop talking guff!" Darnell said, yet again.

"Ah, but it is not at all what you term guff, Herbert, when I assure you that I have repented long and long ago. I have repented to a virtually incredible extent; and I have thus made a peace with my

79

conscience as to every one of those past peccadilloes which you, so to speak, are now planning to season with truisms before flinging in my face. But only, I mean, so far as went that which—speaking tactfully, Herbert, as befits a conference between gentlemen—we may call your grounds, *in articulo mortis*, for becoming angry with me. I cannot pretend to repent—or at any rate, not at all reasonably, you silly-billy!—for having assisted you out of the worries and discomforts of your flesh-and-blood existence, when the police were looking for you, and immediately after you had burst into my room, without even knocking at the door, in order to blow out my brains. You see, Herbert, I value my brains. I have had them ever since I was born. I have become attached to them."

"Yes, but," Darnell said, "but, Diego, I just had to do something or other about it, after I found out how you had been seducing my wife."

He did not really say "seducing," but for propriety's sake one inclines to Latinize the excursus of the ghost, at this special point, into Anglo-Saxon.

Nor did Diego hide his disapproval of any such language. Diego told Herbert Darnell, quite frankly:

"It would be far better taste not to introduce the name of a gentlewoman into this discussion. And when you, the ghost of her own husband, are guilty of any such misdemeanor, I admit to being astonished."

"But the two of you had been fooling me for more than eight months, Diego—"

"And our continuous attempts," Diego replied, "to withhold from your knowledge an affair which, we believed—and believed with justice—would more or less upset your peace of mind, ought never to have been criticized with disfavor by, of all persons, you. Our friendly forethought was not any excuse for your having applied to me epithets such as, in the interests of decency, I decline to repeat. You spoke, you must let me remind you, with the regrettable coarseness of a major prophet. You brandished pistols like a buccaneer in a third-rate historical novel—or at least you brandished one pistol. You observe I am fair-minded. I do not exaggerate the number of pistols which you brandished."

"Stop talking!" the ghost ordered.

"In all other respects I am more than willing to oblige you, Herbert; but I cannot stop talking until after I have fulfilled my duty. For me to stop talking would not be fair to you. It is my most manifest duty, as your personal friend, to point out that you compelled me, through the repugnant but the only possible means which your anger had left available, to prevent you from committing murder—"

"Yah!" said the ghost.

"—Because murder, whenever it is committed by any person who is not wearing a uniform at the time when the murder takes place," Diego reminded Herbert Darnell, "ranks as an acknowledged indiscretion, alike in the twentieth chapter of Genesis, the opinion of Mrs. Grundy, the fifth chapter of Deuteronomy, the story of Bluebeard, the nineteenth chapter of Matthew, verse eighteen, and the criminal code of every state in the union. You yet furthermore put me to the expense of providing both your wife and myself with an alibi. You, in brief, were wholly inconsiderate of everybody's comfort; and I still wonder at the immoderation of your behavior."

"Yes, but, Diego, you and her was pulling wool over my eyes," Darnell persisted, "and when I found out about it, whatever else could I do?"

"I fear," Diego admitted, frankly, "that I cannot answer your question offhand. If only you had asked my advice at the time, I might have suggested some expedient. But as the affair stands, to the very best of my knowledge, and on account of my staying a bachelor, I have not ever had any really considerable amount of wool pulled over my eyes with the tact which graces a competent married woman. So I may not presume to speak as one having authority."

"Yes, but—" said the ghost.

"Please do not interrupt me thus constantly, Herbert. It is not the pink of courtesy, it is not considerate of other people, for anyone to insist upon doing all the talking. I was about to remark, then, I cannot grant that in civilized society any person is entitled, as one or another of our leading writers has phrased it, perhaps Sinclair Lewis or it might have been Longfellow, to take the law into his own hands. Those little hands were never meant to scratch each other's eyes, he goes on to add, to the best of my recollection. You should, instead, have consulted a lawyer."

"Yes, but, you gasbag—!" said the ghost.

"I do not mean a criminal lawyer," said Diego, "such as ordinarily defended you, but a more reputable evader of justice who was employed, upon an annual basis, by large corporations. I mean a lawyer with at least three junior partners and a subdued taste in neckties and a Phi Beta Kappa key. He would have advised you as to the proper legal steps. He would have outlined for you the correct course of conduct which it was your misfortune not to pursue as would have befitted the law-abiding citizen such as, I have to admit with regret, you were not—"

"But—" said Darnell.

"Nevertheless, as I was about to observe, Herbert, when for the fourth or fifth occasion you saw fit to interrupt me, the impropriety of your behavior is a matter which I long since have come to condone. So there is not any call for you to be dwelling thus remorsefully upon your mistakes. You need not even waste time by apologizing for the incivility of your behavior. No, Herbert: let us not confuse the immediate and the only important issue by raking up any more of those ancient blunders upon your part which I have not merely forgiven but have likewise dismissed from reflection."

"Shut up!" said the enraged but now somewhat flustered ghost of Herbert Darnell.

"Let us instead stick to the point," said Diego, equably, "which is that, for some reason or another, you have elected to haunt me. I have had the honor to ask what prompts any such liberty upon your part; and I feel it my duty to insist upon a straightforward reply."

"Why, but I am haunting you," the ghost answered, and Darnell was now speaking in bewilderment, as Diego noted with relief, "because you bumped me off. That was what I ought to do, so they all told me, after you began fooling with magic. And it is you what are not acting right, Diego. Even if you have not got enough sense of decency to be smitten with remorse forever and forever, you ought at any rate to be chilled with horror."

"This sudden elevation in your rhetoric, as well as the claptrap of it," Diego responded, "suggests that not even beyond the tomb is one safe from the corrupting inanities of moving pictures. In any event, if you indeed have been so ill-advised as to leave your grave with no more praiseworthy or more plausible objective in mind than to chill with horror Diego de Arredondo Dodd, then I can but pity the gymnastics of your intelligence. For whatever, to begin with, could you hope to gain by my being chilled with horror?"

"I wanted to get even with you," Darnell grumbled sullenly.

"A desire for revenge is un-Christian, my poor Herbert; and as a former backslider from the Methodist persuasion—or perhaps it was the Baptists whom you obliged—you ought to blush for having harbored it."

"But, Diego—" the ghost protested.

"In fact," Diego conceded generously, "now that I think of it, you had been, so your wife told me, during the earlier and the less criminal part of your flesh-and-blood existence, an Independent Presbyterian. Nor as a ghost, I imagine, are you qualified to blush, I mean, at all perceptibly, upon account

*85*

of your being pearl-colored and vaporous. You observe that I continue to be fair-minded."

"Stop talking!" the ghost wailed.

"So I do not insist," said Diego, "upon your blushing. Yet in either case, and so to speak, alike in your apparitional and your religious capacity, Herbert, the principle remains unchanged. And it is a principle, you must let me tell you, which the mere accident of your being the ghost of a, so to speak, postgraduate Independent Presbyterian does not entitle you to dismiss ignored. In fact," Diego added, with the complacent vagueness of self-conscious virtue, "very far from it!"

"It is you what ought to be blushing," the unreasonable phantom answered, "instead of talking so much guff that I cannot hardly get in one word. That is not right of you, Diego, when I have come out of my grave to chill you with horror. Yes, and so have a lot of the other people you got into trouble, along with my poor wife and me, Diego, on account of your being a fine-looking hellion in those days and about as slick as they make them."

And with that, the outtalked ghost of Herbert Darnell waved angrily toward the Huguenot Cemetery.

"This is more interesting," Diego replied, "than any of your earlier statements. Let us confront these carpers."

*86*

## 11 ॐ

THUS SPEAKING, Diego went to the navel-high plaster-covered wall of the graveyard; and he found that in this place there were many ghosts of persons with whom he had been familiar when he was seeing something of the world at large.

Each one of these ghosts was regarding Diego intently. But they could not speak, he knew, unless Diego spoke first to them; and his nature was too peace-loving for him to be doing that.

Any such action could but lead his rather large spectral audience into making complaints, or indeed into voicing outright incivilities. These ghosts, it was obvious, held biassed and deplorably distorted views as to the part which, when he was young and when he was not, as they failed to remember, an idolater of second thoughts, Diego de Arredondo Dodd had played in their discarded flesh-and-blood existence. They were not being at all broad-minded about a number of affairs which Diego had come, long ago, to appraise without any such smug and embittered lack of charity.

A majority of the ladies present, Diego adjudged from their aspect, as well as from what he considered the logic peculiar to women, were prepared to bring charges of seduction, without pausing rationally for one moment to reflect upon the panting and vigorous pleasure which, at least five times hand running, they had each got out of being seduced. They, instead, were all eager to be rebuking him; and the impatience of Myra Darnell, in particular, to become hortatory, Diego found heart-moving to observe.

Diego inferred that even now she felt it her post-mortem duty to be speaking, as the high-spirited and so sensual, forever squabbling, little brunette monkey used to put it, simply for Diego's own good, and as a warning to Diego not to be lying all the time, now that Myra Darnell could see him standing upon San Marco Avenue in talk with the ghost of her husband. Poor little Myra did not know how much of the truth Diego might be telling her husband. She did not trust Diego, it was evident, to be quite economical enough in his truth-telling.

So Diego waved to her reassuringly. He recalled, with some pride, the mathematical proofs of his once ardent, or to be rather more exact, of Diego's repeatedly ardent affection for Myra; and he then resumed his inspection of the dead, without approving at all cordially of their demeanor.

The ghosts of Jack Chantrey and of Roger Maldahyde, Diego noted, were still judging over-hastily, and from an unbecomingly self-centered point of view, the part which a proper feeling of duty toward Diego's own personal needs had compelled

Diego to play during their final moments as human beings. Old Aubrey Thompson, with a complete lack of that dignity which befits a dead person, was flourishing the ghosts of those two checks about the signatures to which he had behaved so unreasonably. Nor did any other face which at a casual glance Diego could recognize appear to regard him with unflawed affection. These phantoms one and all seemed to think that Diego de Arredondo Dodd had treated them badly, or at any rate that he had fallen short of what they expected of him.

Well, and after a fashion, Diego remained so fair-minded as to see their grievance in each case. There, to the other side, was no single case in which, whenever Diego had felt his conduct to be technically illegal, or even not over well advised, he had not repented for his conduct at the very first moment convenient; but with a long and important journey before him, Diego had not the time, at this instant, to explain about his complete transit into the impeccable. He instead appraised alike the denunciatory and the reproachful relics of Diego's haphazard young manhood with a prudent taciturnity.

"You ought to be begging every one of their pardons right now; and you damn well know it too, Diego," said the outtalked ghost of Herbert

Darnell, which still remained impatiently impor-
tunate at Diego's left elbow.

"My dear, obtuse, absurd poor Herbert!" Diego
protested, without any special ill-will. "You forget
that already I have been so unwise as to speak to
one ghost from out of my past. And if you will
pardon my candor, my reward for being thus polite
was to have you talk at random, with an over-riding of all common-sense logic no less deplorable
than I have found your loquacious unwillingness
to let bygones be bygones. I do not care to unloose
any more such balderdash."

Diego spoke courteously, and lightly enough.
But at bottom he was not merry, now that he faced
the especial ghosts which had been evoked by his
birthstone. He in fact became indignant.

For the magic of this queer green stone, he reflected, was unfairly selective. That in his young
manhood there had been some awkward and perhaps a few rather ugly episodes, Diego granted.
Yes: but then there had been far more in it. There
had been kindliness and bravery and generosity,
and staunch friendships and a number of love affairs about which you could think, well, so to speak,
without any mental fidgeting, and with complete
self-approbation.

Why, but there were scores upon scores, or at
any rate there were several dozens, of yet other

persons with whom he had been familiar when Diego was seeing something of the world at large! and whose ghosts, had they been present, would now be regarding him with a continued good-will and fondness, or even with some gratitude and love. For the boy had been kindly by nature; he quite honestly liked to give pleasure to everybody whenever the cost of this pleasure was not excessive; and so he had acted handsomely enough, he had acted applaudably, in his dealings with almost all his associates. In fact, he had dealt creditably with every one of them—Diego's fretted thinking ran on—except only it might be with these persons whose ghosts you now confronted.

The magic of the queer green stone, in brief, was very much too high-handedly selective. Yet nothing whatever could be done about it, except to pretend that a moderate-minded and well-thought-of citizen was not a bit troubled by its unfairness.

So Diego now looked, affably and patronizingly, down his long Arredondoish-shaped nose, toward these special ghosts which had come out of his past to denounce and to reprove a treasurer of the Laymen's League and a promising candidate for the City Commission. Afterward he bowed low before these ghosts, half jeeringly, he hoped, and yet too, he was certain, with a sort of heartsick desperation.

Then he turned away, as jauntily as could be

managed, from the hatred and from the sorrow and from the scornfulness of these thirty-some ghosts, or it might be a few over forty ghosts, so as to cross San Marco Avenue, and thus to reach the Fort Green.

## 12 ⯎

"Now it was a large while ago," Diego reflected, "and a while which has had in it many changes, since I came to this place with Catherine Mary Zapo in the time of our youthfulness. It seems in fact a fair number of geological eras, since the two of us all-confident and clean-hearted youngsters inspected that faraway castle in the sunset with a placid gaze of proprietorship."

Since he remained at heart a romantic, Diego sighed to think about that remote afternoon. He then dismissed a variety of sentimental reflections in favor of more immediate and practical matters, now that he observed the number of horses which, in a clear twilight, were grazing upon the unevenly mowed grass of the Fort Green.

They were of all sizes and colors, and many of them displayed uncustomary features, for these were the horses of legend and of myths that are older than recorded time. And among them of course one could easily distinguish golden-winged, tall glittering Pegasus, as the herd's leader; and milk-white Borak, because of her eagle wings and her woman's face; and gray Sleipnir, upon account of his having eight legs. The human front legs of Arion, also, and the rear end of Hippocampes, shaped like the tail of a fish, made each of these stallions more or less conspicuous. As for that somewhat out-of-place seeming roan-colored ass, over yonder toward the Castillo's moat, she had been bred, beyond doubt, at Pethor in Midian, where she had once belonged to the prophet Balaam.

And here likewise, all grazing together, so Diego reflected, were Incitatus, and Bayard, and Papillon, and Hrimfaxi, and Bucephalus—for in fact you noticed Bucephalus, a little way to your right hand, because his head resembled that of an ox—as well as the four horses of the Sun, and Aurora's horses, and the two horses of Achilles (both swift-footed Balios and chestnut-colored, over-talkative Xanthos), and the Trojan horse, and the man-eating mares of Diomed, and the dappled mares of the Maruts, and the hobby horse, and the Kelpy.

It was a quite interesting exhibit. You regretted you could not well wait to examine these romance-hallowed steeds, or not with any particularity at least, inasmuch as your present and your far more important concern was with their herdsman.

Now, through a touch of coincidence, such as startled Diego by its strangeness, he found the immortal of whom Diego was in search to be sitting upon the very same bench from which Catherine Mary and Diego had appraised their castle in the sunset—with the difference that this bench, which formerly had been of a rather dark green color, had been repainted gray since then, by the National Park Service, a perceptibly bluish gray.

Well, and the fiend who sat upon this bench was an honest-looking and inconspicuous, gray-bearded, somewhat heavy-set demon. He wore a loosely fitting gray coat, approaching the color of mouse fur; and he wore nothing else except a dark red loincloth. His legs Diego observed to be uncommonly hairy; and the left foot of this evil spirit was shaped in general like the hoof of a goat, only it was considerably larger. The toes of his right foot were stubby; but the toenails were vigorous and undeformed, upon account of his not ever having worn shoes; and they had been trimmed neatly into a pointed clawlike shape.

His appearance, in brief, was not in any way remarkable except for the intentness with which this depraved enemy of mankind's salvation was considering some malefic problem or another. So profound indeed were his meditations that he did not perceive Diego's arrival; and the latter needed to secure the devil's attention with the aid of a light tap between those shoulder blades to which, as Diego found it quaint to remember, the wings of an angel had once been attached.

# 13 ?~

"Sir," Diego began, "even though it be with some agony, or at any rate with a suitable amount of embarrassment, that I disturb your reverie—"

"You have done worse than that," the fiend replied, "for I was composing a rather striking advertisement of Zion. Now you have interrupted the flow of my inspiration; and perhaps I shall not ever recapture it. Whatever is it that you want of me?"

"Since frankness is very often the father of friendship," said Diego, without being so intrusive as to pry into the reasons of any devil for advertising Zion, "I am making bold to request your advice in an affair which is to me of some personal importance."

"And what is this affair?"

"Why, to continue being candid with you, sir, my name is Diego de Arredondo Dodd, and I wish to go to Hell."

"Your desire is unusual," the demon replied, without any least sign of the professional interest such as a right-thinking evil spirit, so Diego felt, ought to have shown toward Diego's project.

"Even so, sir," Diego returned, "my desire to enter the infernal regions is prompted by filial piety."

"Why, then your motive likewise is out of the ordinary, Mr. Something-or-other Dodd, so I believe you said the name was. For I admit that your appellation, although it is no doubt revered in the very highest social circles, has hitherto been to me unfamiliar."

"The misfortune, sir, is mine," Diego responded, politely; "and I grieve likewise that I lack any positive knowledge as to your name, either. Yet I take it that I now have the honor to address his Infernal Highness Asmodeus."

"I have borne many titles, Mr. Dodd; but Asmodeus will serve neatly enough for the dispatch of your business, as to the exact nature of which I as yet stay uninformed."

"Why, but, Mr. Asmodeus, it is merely that I would like to borrow one of your horses. For my foster father has told me over and yet over again that if wishes were horses, then most of us would ride to the devil—"

"That by ill-luck is true," the fiend returned, with a sigh.

"—Whereas my great-aunt, Miss Isabel de Arredondo, sir, has told me that the horses of Asmodeus will carry their bold riders to whatever place the human heart may desire, at its owner's peril."

"Now do you pardon me for a moment," said Asmodeus, in the while that he took out of his breast pocket a black-bound notebook and consulted its pages. He then said:

"Why, but to be sure! Her name in our religion is Pickle-Nearest-the-Wind, and her familiar, I observe, is Ranting Roarer. I can well remember Pickle as a most charming girl, with remarkably captivating freckles. I was privileged to dance with Miss Arredondo, as you term her, at her first Sabbat; and I note that yet other members of her family have dealt with us. You come exceedingly well recommended, Mr. Dodd. And so, for old times' sake, I shall make bold to dissuade you from trying to enter Hell. I do not think the attempt would result happily."

"Your advice astounds me," said Diego, without hiding his disapproval of the fiend's moral laxity, "for to fulfill one's duty is proper in every profession, as almost every one of the World's Forty Great Thinkers has pointed out. I received gratis a copy in four volumes, boxed, from one of my book clubs, you must let me explain, containing a précis of all the philosophies which men have lived by, from Confucius, *circa* 500 B. C., down to Einstein and

Freud and, to the best of my recollection, even down to the prehensile philosophy of a Roosevelt, in our own times. These books enable any literate person to have the wisdom of the ages, not in his head of course, but at his finger tips, which is a location how far more profitable in a democracy! And so, as I was stating, sir, it appears your manifest destiny to entice into Hell as many human beings as you may find possible."

Now the devil shook his head.

"Once, Mr. Dodd, once very long ago, that was the case. But as time passed, we have found it advisable to restrict our clientele."

"I can appreciate the wisdom of that course, Mr. Asmodeus, inasmuch as it is my own professional duty to conduct a tourist home. So I know how careful one has to be about the behavior of one's patrons, and about their smoking in bed and carrying off the face towels, or being really married. I mean, to each other. Nevertheless, sir, ever since the afternoon of my confirmation I have been a staunch Episcopalian. I have left undone the things which I ought to have done; and I have done the things which I ought not to have done. I have thus qualified myself, as the radio announcers put it on Saturday, to attend the church of my choice without committing the sad crime of perjury—as well as, I submit, to enter into Hell, for a brief visit at

*98*

any rate, without any particular affront to Hell's moral standards."

But again Asmodeus shook his gray head. And the fiend told Diego:

"Even so, you have settled down, and you have reformed. You see, Mr. Dodd, our rules are rather strict nowadays. Our rules require that a candidate for admission should reek with infamy. You, instead, if you will condone my frankness, reek with the respectability of a prospering tradesman. I do not question that during your youth you may have been guilty of enough offences to have qualified under the old rules, which were unexigent and catholic as to all forms of misdemeanor. But the rules of Hell have been changed; and for the sake of your esteemed family, upon the Arredondo side, I would not like to see you blackballed because of your recent indulgence in virtue."

Diego sighed; and Diego spoke with dejection, saying:

"I perceive, Mr. Asmodeus, that I should have come to you in the days when, as a friend of mine has lately phrased the affair, just over yonder in the Huguenot Cemetery, I was a fine-looking young hellion and about as slick as they make them. You would then have admitted me without question, I regret to say. But after I had run through the customary indiscretions of youth, such as support loyally our police force and enable our magistrates also to earn a fair salary, I thought it best to repent for these indiscretions and to reform."

"So many of you reason thus, Mr. Dodd; and whither, pray, does such logic conduct you? Why, but more often than not, you reformed sinners end up in the New Jerusalem, and indeed a large number of you have been canonized."

"It is merely that in the days and perhaps even more deplorably during the nights of my youthfulness, Mr. Asmodeus, when I was being guided, without knowing it, by my obligations in the way of correct filial principles, from which I relapsed, as I do not deny, when I repented and became a reformed person—"

"You must not think," the fiend resumed hastily, with a notable air of contrition, "that I would criticize the Holy City with disfavor. Very many of its patrons get pleasure out of its Quaint Old-World Atmosphere; and for people who like that sort of thing, or who care for bathing and all other water sports in its justly famous crystal sea, the Holy City affords an agreeable eternity. You would, I doubt not, be more than satisfied in the New Jerusalem, Mr. Dodd; and any one of the four horses which appeared to St. John at Patmos stands ready to convey you to its pearly gates now that you have reformed and become respectable."

"But if you will pardon me, Mr. Asmodeus, I am trying to tell you that I reformed, and I became respectable, before I had any least notion as to what more stringent and what in fact decalogic obligations had been laid upon me by the demands of filial piety."

Thus speaking, Diego took out of his pocket the queer green stone. And he was about to explain how he came by it, when Diego's diabolical companion said, with a sudden change of demeanor:

"This very much alters matters. This relieves me of the distasteful need to voice any more tarradiddles; and it likewise compels me to ask for a repeating of your name, or rather, of your Christian name, my dear fellow, so that we may dispense with formality."

"I am still called, sir, Diego de Arredondo Dodd."

"Why, then, Diego, I must tell you that the father whom you desire to visit is my father also—the dissolute young scamp!" Asmodeus added, with affection.

## 14 &

Now, with a continued air of affection, the fiend embraced Diego. For, as Asmodeus went on to explain, this Asmodeus was the son of Adam's first wife, Lilith; and had been begotten toward the conclusion of that fortnight which Lilith and her husband spent happily together in the Garden of Eden, after their joint creation, by Jehovah, upon the sixth day of September in the year 4004 B. C. The ardor of their mutual fondness throughout this fortnight was unexampled. But upon the twentieth day of September, toward four o'clock in the afternoon, Red Samaël, who was then a seraph, led Lilith away from the warm sunlit paths of Eden, into the refreshing shade of a huge tree which thrived in the midst of this garden, and away from the paths of virtue also.

Because of this indiscretion Lilith was cast out of Eden; and a yet further result of her indiscretion, some three-quarters of a year later, was Asmodeus. And as a reproach to Adam for having neglected Lilith during that warm afternoon, one of his ribs was promoted to become for him an ever-present rod of correction. But Eve had spoken corrosively with Adam for rather less than a fortnight before her quietness on a sudden was noticeable, and thus aroused the curiosity of Jehovah.

"So yet again Jehovah looked down toward Eden," said Asmodeus; "and yet again He perceived in the midst of this fair garden our father's rump, which no tree, howsoever widespread its branches or thick its foliage, could hide from the gaze of omniscience. And Jehovah rebuked our father for continuing in this way to usurp the tender privileges which had been meant for Adam alone."

Red Samaël remained unrepentant.

"Why, O Creator of us all, should I, whom You made of fire, be considering a creature whom You made of mud?" the seraph argued. "I am the far better fitted to keep Your Garden of Eden a continual paradise for his wives, as either one of them will now assure You. For it is the nature of mud to become sodden and to collapse; but a fire, O Lord God of Sabaoth, when once it is kindled, and has fuel before it, stays forever resurgent."

Jehovah then became very angry at this criticism of Adam's shortcomings, because no creative artist can bear to be told that his current compositions are inferior to his early work. Jehovah said,—

"It shall be your punishment, Red Samaël, as the first of all art critics, that the fire in you, which is called youth, shall not ever be extinguished."

Thus spoke the Lord God of Sabaoth in anger; and as was customary, His speaking became a law. It is upon account of this law that all art critics continue to be despised by religious persons; and that Red Samaël alone of created beings has retained his youth and his youth's restlessness, along with his partiality for the favorite recreations of youth.

"—As a result of which partiality," said Asmodeus, in conclusion, "nobody can pretend to say how many heroic and turbulent male children our father has begotten with the aid of earth's lovelier women in all eras. Cain was of course the first of his mortal sons; then Esau; and after these followed a number of yet other Biblical and historic persons, whom here to enumerate might entrench upon the tedious. And with every one of his newborn sons it is the generous-hearted custom of the young rascal to leave the carved green stone by which he may recognize them when they come to him to get their desire."

"This is indeed abhorrent news," said Diego, with a correct air of melancholy, "for a person of my responsible civic and social position to be hearing about his own father. And it is doubly distressing news, brother Asmodeus, because of my position's compelling me to honor any such father. For I am neither heroic nor turbulent any longer. I nowadays am instead an Episcopalian, a Kiwanian, an Elk, and a member of the Chamber of Commerce as well as of the Hotel Men's Association, in addition to being a vestryman and the treasurer of our Laymen's League. So it really would not do for me to be taking liberties with the fifth commandment, or with any other part of the Decalogue, such as people might hear about."

Now Diego's infernal half-brother nodded with an aspect of complete and in fact of some sympathetic comprehension, when he had been made aware of Diego's various social and religious affiliations. And Asmodeus said, condoningly:

"You came to believe, in short, after youth's fire had gone out of you, that toward middle-age, men ought to become thrifty and prudent; and that an intelligent person, through the exercise of these and of all other virtues such as may prove convenient, ought to avoid the discomforts of Hell."

"That, speaking generally, brother Asmodeus, I take to be an approved doctrine of every known branch of the Christian faith; and as such I had accepted it."

"Such likewise," returned Asmodeus, "is the doctrine of Hell. The large difference is that we infernal spirits are far less lukewarm than are you Christians as to the importance of your faith, upon which depends our country's welfare. But do you be seated, my dear brother Diego, so that in comfort and with rather more complete leisure I may explain to you about this matter."

## 15 ஃ

IT WAS somewhat less a matter (Asmodeus continued) of pietistic principles, or of altruism, than of mathematics. At the time of Satan's rebellion, nearly seven and a half million angels had left Heaven in order to seek freedom of religion; they established new homes among the untamed virgin conflagrations of Hell; and because of their industry all prospered with these pioneers of an elective system of government and of a more liberal way of living than had been permitted to them under the autocracy of Jehovah.

Untiringly, these devoted and staunch-hearted devils tempted mankind into disregarding the primitive notions of their celestial Adversary. They continued to do this even after a major part of the rather too drastic commandments handed down from Mount Sinai had been amended and made more tactful by the charitableness of Christianity. And daily more and more human beings from all quarters of earth succumbed to the snares set for them by demons; so that after death these sinners became damned souls.

Hell in this manner thrived and was enriched through its founders' industry. It by-and-by had been enriched with so many lost souls that the devils had more labors imposed upon them, in the way of cookery and of vivisection and of yet other torments, than they could well attend to without personal inconvenience. These labors permitted them no idleness. The fiends had left to them hardly a vacant moment during which to seek recreation. Far less had they the time for an outing during which to entice yet more human beings into becoming damned. For this reason, they discontinued their evil wiles.

But the devils found that men, of their own accord, and with the agile co-operation of many women, went on breaking Jehovah's commandments; and that as the human race increased in numerousness, more and more persons died and were damned. The hosts of lost souls thus became too large to be dealt with by only 7,450,926 tormentors—which was the exact number of devils in Hell, so Asmodeus told Diego, after yet again the fiend had consulted his black notebook.

Nor was there now any question of making the damned suffer. The problem, now, was to find room in Hell for Hell's victims, inasmuch as the confines of Hell, while extensive, were also inelastic.

In this national crisis, Satan assembled the seventy-two princes of Hell, and they all took counsel together.

Lucifer, the Lord Chief Justice, spoke first, pointing out that the housing problem defied solution except through some radical change of infernal policy—the nature of which change, the speaker continued, it was far from his intention to suggest, inasmuch as he could think of no plain way out of their present troubles.

"Meanwhile," said Lucifer, "we have no more vacancies. Our torture chambers, our bonfires, our furnaces, and even the incinerators which were planned to dispose of our waste paper and our garbage, are filled to repletion by the damned. Yet in the very moment I speak, gentlemen, more and yet more sinners are dying upon earth, even, if I may so venture to express the Gordian knot which we confront, from China to Peru; and for them also we are supposed to provide accommodations and unending torments. It is not possible for us to meet this obligation. We face a state of affairs without any parallel in Hell's history."

Then Rimmon spoke. As the Ambassador to Russia, he was more completely in touch with modern ideas than was the conservative Lord Chief Justice; and Rimmon spoke briskly.

"I must question," said Rimmon, "your employment of the word 'obligation.' Who, when one comes to consider this matter, has laid upon us any obligation to be tormenting these sinners because, like us, they have broken the laws of Jehovah? For us to be doing that is, in fact, not logical."

"Logic is rarely involved in a point of honor," replied Belphegor, who at this time was Envoy Extraordinary to France. "Jehovah has willed that all human beings should keep His laws and thus earn admission into Heaven. When we went into rebellion against Him, it became with us a point of honor to thwart His will in this matter, as in all other matters, and to persuade human beings to reject His laws."

"It was natural that we should tantalize Him in this way," said Rimmon, "even though, to my opinion, our behavior was childish. Yet it does not follow that because we wished to prevent human beings from ascending into Heaven, we should have permitted them to enter Hell."

Here was a point which the devils had not considered earlier; and murmurs of astonishment, of doubt and of approval ran confusedly about the assembly. A half-dozen or so of fiends began to applaud; and one of these now arose and spoke. He was Verdelet, the Master of Ceremonies.

"I agree with Rimmon," said Verdelet, "that by acting upon a *non sequitur*, if I may so phrase it, gentlemen, we have incurred many arduous responsibilities. The state of damnation is not without serious inconveniences for a demon, in that he enjoys so very little leisure."

"We enjoy no leisure whatever," said Belial. "Never since I quitted Heaven have I found a moment which I could call my own. When I am not tempting some human being into mortal error, I have to be torturing some damned soul or another."

"And besides, gentlemen, in order to ensure that these tortures are administered with competence," said the Lord High Chancellor, Adramalech, "we are forced to inhabit a labyrinth of miseries. For, as I do not question many of you may have noticed with disapproval, we live nowadays, and we have lived now for centuries, among perpetual and unquenchable flames, among pitch and brimstone, among smoke and stinks and the screaming of the damned. We have chosen these unattractive surroundings in which to labor, day in and day out, with our firebrands and racks and tweezers and caldrons and muck forks, because of a point of honor. I am not certain we chose wisely."

Then Baalberith said, with deliberation: "More than once I have reflected that, even though the principles of democracy which led us into rebellion against an absolute and perpetual monarch were correct in theory, yet in practice they have caused us to become the slaves of damned souls. We devote our existence to furthering their discomfort. We were better off, it may be, when as cherubim and angels and archangels and seraphim, we lived in serene and high-minded idleness as attendants upon Jehovah."

"In fact, we were rarely required to do more than to hymn His praises," said Nergal. "It was monotonous, and it went against my conscience also, upon account of my not ever very much caring for music, and my belief that no chief executive should be allowed to hold office forever. Yet, as I recall the affair, that period of our downtrodden and inhibited youth, when we were all blessed spirits in Heaven, was less disagreeable, by and large, than we are finding an eternity spent, in one way or another, wholly among human beings."

"And it goes against my conscience nowadays, as the keeper of Hell's gateway," Misroch declared explosively, "to have to be admitting them into our country. I confess, since candor may be the shortest road out of our difficulties, that I cannot applaud Hell's entomology, in collecting the most detestable vermin which Jehovah has created."

"Ah, but, my friends, it is the principle of the thing—" Satan began.

"Moreover," Red Samaël the Seducer protested, with a grave young smile which reminiscence flavored, "the female of this vermin, as Misroch calls the human race, are far from being detestable when they are properly upset."

"We know your record as to earth's women," Satan replied sternly, "and the less which is said about it, before a council of self-respecting devils, the better. As I was telling you, my friends"— Satan bleated out, benevolently, addressing the princes in general—"it is the principle of the thing which must be considered. We rebelled, and we seceded from the Kingdom of Heaven, in order that in defiance of Jehovah's effete monarchical system of government, we might establish our independence—"

"And as I was telling you, Mr. President," Belial broke in, with a hint of sharpness, "we instead have established our slavery. We live in servitude to a point of honor. Personally, I have not anything against honor so long as it is confined to private life. In public life it is out of place. For any nation to be influenced by considerations of honor, as Hell alone among nations has ever been influenced, is to invite confusion and discomfort. I do not like confusion and discomfort. For this reason I agree with Rimmon. We erred when we admitted human beings into Hell. And it is the part of common-sense for us to confess our error."

Then Chamos said, with conviction: "His Excellency the Minister to Turkey has spoken wisely.

We should not any longer tolerate the requirements of human beings. Hell needs to be humanized."

"I must call upon the Grand Chamberlain," said
Satan, not slenderly puzzled, "to explain his last
remark."

"It has been our mistake, Mr. President,"
Chamos replied, "to regard mankind as being but
so many counters in the game which we played
against Jehovah. He has won a small number of
these counters, and we, as our present difficulty
well testifies, have won a huge number. Meanwhile, we have not paused to observe the doings
of mankind in the way of such abominations as did
not violate the tenets of the Christian faith—nor,
as I make haste to add, the tenets of the Jewish
faith either, because many of our best friends have
been Jews—"

"In fact," said Satan, "Hell would not be Hell if
ever we had permitted any such racial discrimina-
tions as are practised among human beings. Nevertheless, you have not as yet explained your sug-
gestion that Hell needs to be humanized."

"I mean," said Chamos, "that much may be
gained by a philosopher through study of the lower
forms of life, even through a study of men and
women. Nobody except only our young frivolous
brother Samaël disputes that they are trivial and

repulsive creatures. Yet we ought to admit, fair-mindedly, that these human beings have developed an inhumanity which Hell lacks, and by observing which we may now profit. Their wars have begotten among such of these human beings as are Christians, in their pursuit of human brotherhood, a number of creditable and ingenious discoveries such as no devil had ever thought about."

"I admit that the Christian nations have upset our former notions of warfare," said Satan, with a gesture of distaste, "through the discovery made by their department stores, in conjunction with the pastors of these Christians, that no soldier who goes into battle wearing a small steel-covered Bible over his heart will ever be injured in battle. Nor do I question the highly practical value of this discovery. Yet I do not think it would be honorable for us to profit by this discovery in our war with Heaven. My views are perhaps old-fashioned," Satan admitted, "but I feel that no self-respecting devil, while on military duty, should defend his person with a Bible in this underhand fashion. It is the principle of the thing, my friends."

"But you mistake my meaning, Mr. President," said Chamos. "I allude, rather, to the convenient idea of national displacement. I refer to the discovery that all such of one's enemies as one fails to destroy may be got rid of just as handily by evicting them from the country which they inhabit. And so, Mr. President, I propose that the damned shall be treated henceforward in a more rational and human manner. I propose that the damned shall be displaced from their homes in Hell, where they have become to us an affliction."

Then one of the minor princes, whose name the Clerk did not obtain, asked,—

"But where will they go?"

"By all the rules of humanity," Chamos replied, "that is a problem for which displaced persons are left free to find the answer themselves. Ordinarily, of course, the displaced citizens of a nation, in common with the other citizens of that nation, are maintained in comfort by the credulity of the United States of America. Nor do I question that in our fellow democracy the first political party to demand, upon humanitarian grounds, an unrestricted immigration of damned souls from out of Hell, in common with all other persecuted or displaced or undesirable persons from everywhere else, will, as our American imitators phrase it, sweep the country. That, however, is not our affair. The true point is that by displacing the damned we shall be rid of our housing problem; we shall be spared the discomfort and the labor of tormenting the damned; and for the first time in Hell's history all we infernal spirits shall live at ease."

Loud cheers interrupted the speaking of Chamos. Rimmon seconded the motion, and it was carried. High-minded Satan alone objected to the principle of the thing, which he declared to be a repudiation of Hell's famousness for hospitality; but his protest went unheeded now that the other devils could see comfort within their reach.

## 16 ε∾

EIGHT and one-half trillions of damned souls (so did Asmodeus continue his narrative) were then evicted from Hell daily. Their exodus from Hell was enforced at this uniform rate every day, to the best of Asmodeus' recollection, throughout two solar years and four months hand running; Hell was thus freed from its victims; the fires of Hell were extinguished; and the displaced damned were left adrift among various planetary systems.

Whatever did become of these vagabonds in the upshot, Asmodeus could not tell Diego. No fiend had ever been at pains to inquire about that particular triviality. The important point was that Hell was now rid of all the damned except only those who had been notable architects or successful moving picture directors during their lives upon earth. All these were retained in order that by their genius Hell might be rebuilded throughout, gaily and luxuriously, in technicolor, with a fine palace for every demon.

Moreover, in several respects Hell's foreign policy was revised. A committee of infernal princes, with Asmodeus as chairman, and consisting in all of nine members, was appointed to erect, alongside the Highway of the Dead, a number of billboards which would instruct every deceased traveler as to the attractions and accessibility of the paradises of each current religion, a slight distance farther on; and which in this way would induce the dead to pass by the gates of Hell without bothering anybody. And it was voted unanimously by the seventy-two princes that the relinquished practice of tempting mankind would be resumed, with the difference that, henceforward, all demons, so often as they found time for it, would tempt mankind to live virtuously; to avoid every form of sin; and thus to keep out of Hell.

In order to preserve Hell's national honor—or as Satan phrased it, "for the principle of the thing"— the infernal regions must still pretend to carry on, under the staid oriflamme of "Business as Usual," their former economic activities. But in point of fact, the devils were living at ease, in their new palaces, without having any more heavy obligations laid upon them than in a gentlemanly and friendly fashion to encourage among mankind a tactful humoring of Jehovah's least whim. And they refused to admit even the most depraved sinner, nowadays, upon the ground that his iniquity had not been of a nature sufficiently striking to conform with the moral standards of Hell's clientele.

"About these matters I may tell you, my dear brother Diego," Asmodeus ended, "since it is all in the family. The green stone will procure your admission into Hell, when once you have showed it to Misroch; and whichever one of my horses you may prefer is at your disposal, to convey you into the presence of our infernal father."

"I elect then, brother Asmodeus, for that stallion yonder which is colored like silver and is wearing a golden bridle."

It was a choice as to which Asmodeus demurred. The fiend said, warningly:

"That silver stallion which used to ramp in Poictesme, my dear Diego, is nowadays an infirm and discredited animal. He has seen much service; and between ourselves, those veterinarians whose opinions as to æsthetic matters are just at present viewed seriously, tell me that he is ill-constructed and weak-knee'd, in addition to having been overridden."

"Nevertheless, brother Asmodeus, that timetried stallion will serve my purpose; for in middle life one prefers to ride quietly, and to perceive, toward the end of the journey, that one is being jostled by no competitors who might call for envy."

"Very well, then," said Asmodeus, with a slight shrug.

He told Diego in what manner Diego could reach most quickly the Highway of the Dead. After that, Diego thanked Asmodeus for his civility; the half-brothers embraced yet again; and Diego mounted the silver stallion.

Diego then rode away from the Fort Green, leaving behind him the Quaint and Progressive City of St. Augustine, as the Chamber of Commerce calls it: but he did not ride either toward Jacksonville or in the direction of Vilano Beach. Nor, for that matter, did the silver stallion see fit to turn westward toward Picolata and the St. Johns River, now that a thrifty-minded sense of filial duty had made the destination of Diego de Arredondo Dodd infernal.

*Part Four* ॐ

# IN LANDS BEYOND COMMON-SENSE

*"Behold I . . . will keep thee in all places whither thou goest, and will bring thee again into this land."*

—GENESIS, XXVIII, 15

# 17 ॐ

IT IS my next need to tell you that the direction in which Diego traveled after leaving the Fort Green did not ever become a matter of record, because Diego thought it would be unworthy of him to assist his fellow creatures in reaching Hell. He knew from his own experience, in conducting the Bide-A-While Tourist Home, how awkward it is to have to turn away undesired patrons.

So Diego felt it his filial duty, as well as a matter of professional courtesy, upon account of his being a member of the Hotel Men's Association, for him not to aid the general public in annoying the proprietors of Hell with a demand for accommodations, now that his family upon his father's side, as Diego phrased the affair, were endeavoring to conduct a strictly first-class year-round resort by excluding from it the souls of the damned. When you came to think about this matter, Diego's conscience told him, damned souls were not the sort of patrons whom he himself would care to have as paying guests at the Bide-A-While Tourist Home, not even overnight, and far less for eternity.

We do know, however, that the silver stallion carried Diego through the Marches of Antan, and across Mispec Moor, into Poictesme, where Diego had a glimpse of Naimes and Aigremont and Asch and Storisende. In Storisende he observed with interest the former castle of Manuel the Redeemer, which was now used as a post office. Just east of Storisende, Diego was delayed by meeting a nightmare in a receptive condition, but the stallion settled that.

Diego then entered Megaris; and so came into yet other irrational countries such as Melphé and Rorn and Ecben, all which the present age has forgotten so completely that in the maps of no atlas are these countries accorded their unmoral latitude and benign coloring.

And when he was asked about present-day conditions in these parts, Diego said there was not any up-to-date or really complete summary to be had anywhere.

"But," he continued, with his thumbs in his armpits, and speaking in that man-of-the-world manner with which he made it a point to embellish his reports as treasurer of the Laymen's League, "American investments in these countries have aggregated over $404,000,000, according to the Department of Commerce, of which direct business investments (in about 100 firms, largely in Garian and Arleoth) were $62,000,000; investments in Rorn corporations, $139,000,000—"

"To think of that, now!" said his hearers.

"—In Ecben Government securities," Diego continued, "$161,000,000; in personal property (mares'-nests, borrowed plumes, Spanish castles, fiddlesticks, Hibernian bulls, ingannations, etc.), $1.37; and in municipal securities (Sorram, Achren, Druim, etc.), $42,000,000."

—Which was no doubt true, inasmuch as Diego after he reached middle life did not very often tell lies unnecessarily; and which at all events, sounded instructive.

Then, after he had come into Rorn, Diego passed through Tarba into the city of Garian, along the same road, so they report, which proud Charlemagne followed when this emperor ventured into the lands beyond common-sense; with the difference that, after leaving the national highway at Garian, instead of taking the dirt road to the north, as did Charlemagne in preference to braving the reputed magic of the forest of Branlon, Diego traveled straight onward.

Here we touch mystery. For I have heard, at first hand, that in this forest Diego met the same Mr. Smith who, it may be remembered, had no less casually than callously espoused and abandoned Catherine Mary Zapo; and that this Mr. Smith turned out to be a woodland deity, with a sorceress for his current wife, who was called Tana.

Yet if any such improbability indeed happened, Diego, upon account of his high respect for Mrs. Catherine M. Smith's social position, appears not ever to have discussed the affair with anybody else, and my friendship for pompous, cautious-minded Diego forces me to respect his confidence.

To other persons Diego reported merely that the fine timber lands between Rorn and Ecben were very well worth visiting.

"In fact," said Diego, in the common-sense manner which he employed at a Chamber of Commerce meeting, "the present value of standing timber in the forest of Branlon is estimated at $480,000,000."

"And whoever would have thought it!" some of his hearers would exclaim.

But the rest of them said, "And that simply shows you!"

"Of the forest lands," Diego continued, "some are owned by professional wizards and companies having saw mills, pulp mills, paper mills, etc. About 90 per cent of the sawn and planed wood is exported, 70 per cent of the wood pulp, and 60 per cent of the paper as it is specially prepared for romance writing."

"Dear me!" said the vestrymen; and they religiously tried their very best not to yawn.

"Pine, ebony, fir, redwood, mahogany, and other valuable cabinet woods," Diego explained also, "are produced here, in addition to magic and much cedar wood for the manufacture of cigar boxes."

"And it is a comfort, Brother Dodd," his fellow Elks would declare, resignedly, under the unending downpour of Diego's instructiveness, "to be hearing so many really important facts about an enchanted forest such as the old fairy tales make it a rule to leave out."

"All rules are like pie crust," said Diego, "in that now and then the wise break them, but not too often."

Well, and after that, Diego came out of Branlon into Arleoth, where a cantilever bridge, which Diego said was a noteworthily inferior copy of the Bridge of Lions at St. Augustine, led over the river Amio, and toward the city of Miradol. This was the capital city of Ecben, where the Träsc has his palace—which is builded of coquina stone, in the very best Spanish Mission style, like the Recreational Center and Tourist Club of St. Augustine, so Diego reported—and where the Czac and the Hrohof hold their assemblies.

"For Ecben," Diego said, in just that jaunty but informative manner with which he devastated the weekly luncheons of his Kiwanis Club, "is now governed, under a Constitution adopted April 13, 1929, by a two-chamber legislative body—"

"There is nothing whatever like being accurate," said all his fellow members of the St. Augustine Historical Society and Institute of Science, with admiration, "except only, just now and then, when any one of us gets to writing about the antiquities of St. Augustine, and when being accurate as to these antiquities would not help the tourist trade."

"—Consisting," said Diego, "of a Senate (Czac) of 111 members and a House (Hrohof) of 444 members, elected by universal suffrage, in a method which takes care of minorities through an efficient jail system."

"—Which," said every one of the attendant Business and Professional Men, "is exactly what we need here in Florida, what with those Republicans getting out of hand."

And then Diego, although he was not talking about Florida of course, or about any other part of the United States of America, but was still being informative as to the present customs of Ecben, went on to say:

"Freedom of speech, press, religion, companionate marriage, judicial bribery, birth control, etc., is guaranteed. The President (Träsc) is elected, upon a commercial basis, by the Parliament

(Wonil) for as long as the public can be deluded by him. Everything, in short, has been modernized most gratifyingly in this former kingdom of dreams."

"For we live nowadays," said his audience, with approval, "in an age of progress."

"Yes," said Diego; "and in fact the *St. Augustine Record* had an editorial about it only last Sunday."

So then did Diego de Arredondo Dodd, in his middle life, a good while after the fire of youth had gone out of him, pass through Poictesme and Megaris and Melphé and Rorn and Ecben, and a number of adjacent countries; and such were his businesslike reports as to the lands beyond common-sense. For not until after he had traversed these magic-infested countries, and had put behind him all their affairs, in common with the injudicious concerns and the over-lofty notions of his youth's rampageousness, might Diego reach the Highway of the Dead, upon which all persons who have not merited the felicities of Heaven are doomed to journey out of mortal living, toward Hell.

## 18 ઇ✢

Now the broad level road passed onward rigidly, without ever faltering to have in it any lenient least bends; and no crossroads entered the Highway of the Dead. To each side of the highway rose a forest. Here and there you saw in it unruffled shallow pools of water, and lilies grew in some of these pools. But in the unending tall forest you observed no birds, except just once when, to the right-hand side of the road, Diego noticed five turkey buzzards eating what remained of a swollen black sow. Nor did the branches of the trees, or even one leaf, move at all, so far as Diego could detect, in the while that Diego rode forward, mounted upon the silver-collored stallion and riding bareback.

He knew that along with him traveled the souls of many dead persons, but to him they remained imperceptible, and so with them he had no concern. He regretted that he no doubt was riding straight into and through the ghosts of men and women and children, in a fashion which, to the deceased ladies in particular, must appear impolite; yet this incivility he could not avoid; and after all, it would not injure, materially, an impalpable spirit.

Moreover, all these lately dead persons, in the while that they journeyed toward Hell, must now be reading the billboards to each side of the highway with far too much interest to be bothering about his violation of traffic laws. For the dead among whom Diego rode stolidly would not know, of course, as Diego knew, that devils had erected every one of these deceiving, gay signs, so as to entice the dead into passing beyond the gates of Hell, in an effort to reach the unending bliss which these signs promised; and thus to be ensnared into wandering about forever, among unfamiliar constellations, at a safe distance from the Solar System, without having upset the comfort of Hell's proprietors.

Now I must tell you these were billboards of which Diego observed the not wholly Biblical wording with reprobation, upon account of his being a vestryman.

"Let your next stop be in the Holy City," so did the first sign exhort the deluded dead. "Entirely remodeled. Everything for a satisfying eternity. New décor. Comfortable beds with Sweet-Slumber Innerspring mattresses. All sports. Friendly service. Orchestra and cocktail lounge. Churches of every denomination near by."

And a second sign proclaimed: "Faith's most distinguished paradise lies just ahead. Take the eternity you have dreamed of in picturesque Zion, high in interplanetary space, away from humming highways, in your own celestial mansion, steam-heated. Informal atmosphere, with every recreational facility. No marriage or giving in marriage. Lots doing."

But the next sign said, rather more austerely: "Spend your second life in the New Jerusalem. A superior seashore home away from home for the discriminating dead. Our milk is grade Double-A. Honey from our own apiaries. A radio in every room. Fireproof. American-Jewish cuisine."

In brief, Diego found the Highway of the Dead a familiar-looking thoroughfare in that, in general essentials, it did not differ from the state highways of his native Florida. And as a vestryman, he could not approve of this similarity. He, as a vestryman, felt that whenever anybody needed to talk about Heaven, it sounded far better to be more grandiloquent and more obsolete and more upliftingly vague in one's language; and thus to avoid, with the loyalty of a confirmed pewholder, ever raising the question, just how deeply would a rational person like to be imprisoned in the Heaven promised by the prospectus of the Protestant Episcopal Church?

It followed that the vestryman part of Diego found these billboards to be ill-advised.

And yet too, as the part owner of a tourist home, Diego adjudged the fact to be gratifying that, when these signs were erected, the committee of nine demons, of which his half-brother Asmodeus was the chairman, should have profited thus unmistakably through the committee's study of those special inducements and the rapid-fire rhetoric which are customary, throughout the United States of America, in promoting the tourist trade.

Diego thus traveled toward Hell in a jumble of anonymous sentiments which stayed almost exactly divided, with somewhat the effect of a barbecue sandwich, so Diego reflected. And he found Hell to be surrounded by a wall which, with a continuing Floridian resemblance, was builded of coquina stone, and which was so tall that Diego, no matter how far he leaned backward, could not see to the top of it.

There was in this wall but one opening, in the form of an arched broad gateway, above which a neon sign, in the bland twilight which had encompassed Diego ever since he passed through the City Gates of St. Augustine, displayed in green the word "usual"; and higher than that, in blue, the word "as"; and still farther up, in red, the word "business." But the two doors of the gateway, which were made of paneled maple wood, stayed closed; and upon the brass door knob to Diego's left hand, suspended by a loop of brown twine, hung a white placard upon which was printed, with a black lettering, "Sorry No Vacancies." All this notice was in capital letters.

The Highway of the Dead passed by and beyond

the inhospitable locked gates. To the mottled and striated, huge gray wall—which rather reminded you, so Diego reflected, of pâté de foie gras—were affixed a number of crudely colored, large paper posters, which depicted, in an excitative modernized vein, the unending delights of Jehovah's heaven, as well as of the heavens of yet other religious faiths; and which mentioned, more or less veraciously, the distance that each one of these eternal last homes lay beyond the gateway of Hell.

"It is evident," Diego thought, "that my brother Asmodeus spoke somewhat more truthfully than do these circus-like, pious posters; and that Hell at long last has become a large deal too intelligent to accommodate immoral and loose-living persons."

He shrugged then, saying to Diego de Arredondo Dodd in private, and without being so imprudent, of course, as to say any word of it aloud:

"Here again, as the manager of a tourist home, I cannot but applaud Hell's wholly proper new restrictions. For I myself practise them. Yet this is an outcome which upsets the cornerstone of every known form of religion; because nobody, so it would seem, is now going to be punished perpetually, except only up to the very last half-second of his mortal life, for not having fallen in with the notions of his neighbors. And as a communicant, I cannot ever approve of any such slack heresy."

## 19 ᛒ᷎

NEVERTHELESS, Diego dismounted from the silver stallion. He rang the electric bell he found to his right hand; and in the closed gateway a barred small wicket opened.

Gaunt, black-haired Misroch, the Chief Steward, looked through this wicket; and with unhidden surprise he asked what Diego meant by approaching the fiery pit of Hell riding on horseback and with the face of a bridegroom.

"Why, but my need is that of a bridegroom," said Diego, "for I wish to get in."

"And at any other time you would be welcome to our most complicated and ingenious torments," Misroch returned civilly. "But at this special instant, as this sign assures you with regret, we have no vacancies. In view of this sad accident, my advice to you is to go forward into Jehovah's Holy City—"

"Nevertheless," Diego began, "it so happens that I have not any present concern with Jehovah—"

"Why, but in that case," said Misroch, "you have merely to ride on nine miles and a half farther in order to reach that Garden of Delight which was designed by Mahommed, Lord of All Apostolic Men; and which is conducted most efficiently, I can assure you, by Allah the Compassionate."

"Yes, but," said Diego, "as an Episcopalian, I am

not allowed to deal with any gods except Mammon and Jehovah."

"For its every patron," said Misroch, "upon lofty couches covered with red damask and arranged within a convenient distance of one another, under the ever-blooming lotus trees of this garden, are provided forty concubines."

"Your statistics shock me," said Diego.

"Each one of these high-bosomed houris," said Misroch, "you will find to be more beautiful than is the moon at its full; and the virginity of each damsel whom you may honor with your caresses, sir, you will be finding, likewise, to renew itself immediately after you have removed it."

"One may very well deplore the morality of these tourist camps," Diego replied. "And as for my being bothered nowanights with forty concubines, I fear that, what with the years of my life also having entered into their forties, the notion had better remain academic."

"Then, but two miles farther along the Highway of the Dead," Misroch resumed ingratiatingly, "stands Elysium. Why, sir, do you not put up, just for eternity, with Elysium's regions of joy, its delightful green retreats, and its blessed abodes in groves where happiness abounds?"

"Because I finished once and for all with Latin," said Diego, "when I got a diploma with my name on it. That is a recognized principle in the education of every American. And so, if only you will stop interrupting me—"

"The hospitable and courteous proprietors of this strictly first-class resort," said Misroch, "have their own sun, their own stars, including a number of the most popular figures in moving pictures. Some of the patrons of Elysium exercise their limbs on the grassy green, others contend in healthful outdoor sports, and wrestle on the tawny sand; some strike the ground with their feet and sing hymns. In fact, Orpheus and his famous swing band have been engaged permanently."

"The preferred music of my youth," said Diego, stubbornly, "was jazz. And I am well past the age for athletics."

"Moreover," said Misroch, "the clientele of Elysium is uncommonly select. There may be seen Teucer's ancient race, a most illustrious line, magnanimous heroes born in happier times. Among the year-round patrons of Elysium are Ilus, Assaracus, and Dardanus, who founded Troy, with yet many other well-known socialites too numerous to mention. I am wholly certain, sir, that you would be more than pleased by Elysium."

"I shall not dispute your most generous, if not unfamiliar, tribute to what was once a rival establishment," Diego returned. "For at the Ketterlinus

High School, I too once studied the regrettable *Æneid* of that same Virgil from whom you are now plagiarizing. To the other side, even though I was once a scholar, I was never a sybarite. It is not for eternal bliss I am seeking, but for my scamp of a father."

"Aha!" said Misroch, with a more lively interest, "and can it be that this is yet another one of you? What, sir, may be the name of your father?"

"I regret to inform you he is called Red Samaël the Seducer, since it perforce rends the heart of a vestryman for his own father to be having any such name. In any case, I am Diego de Arredondo Dodd, from the Quaint and Progressive City of St. Augustine; and here is my birthstone."

Thus speaking, Diego exhibited the queer green stone; and as when india-rubber at the end of a pencil passes over a memorandum made by the leaden point of that pencil, so now from the gaunt, furrowed face of dark-haired Misroch was removed inhospitality. The wicket became tenantless. The gateway of Hell swung open.

Then the Chief Steward of these exclusive regions appeared smilingly, and his harsh face beamed in the while that Misroch shook hands with Diego, and declared:

"You are heartily welcome, Mr. Dodd. I will take you straight to the young rascal."

## 20 &

So was it that Diego came with Misroch, along the broad highways of remodeled Hell, to a white stone palace surmounted by twenty-seven towers, of which the domes were covered with green copper. Round about this palace was the well-shaded tranquillity of a garden planted with twenty-seven kinds of fruit trees and surrounded by a nine feet high railing of golden pillars interknotted with green copper triangles and broken irregularly by twenty-seven gates of brass. About the walkways of this garden went all-glorious seeming, tall young men; and with each one of them walked two or three girls who had comely faces.

When Diego approached, they were all singing together, saying:

"There is none more worthy of praise than is Red Samaël; for Samaël is pre-eminent among immortal beings. He is the most amiable of evil spirits. May the huge-hearted and tawny-haired and forever young demon grant to us eternal shelter in the good-will of Samaël the bounteous giver, he that gave life and turbulence to each one of us!

"To the lustrous-eyed and stalwart dispenser of happiness we send forth a song of praise. We adore the radiant demon with grateful hearts. He is tireless and unresting; strength is inseparable from the Seducer, alike in counsel and in bedrooms; he is deserving of our affection because he is kindly toward the turbulence of each one of us.

"For this reason do we praise the fair and ever-youthful demon, who at need is like an untamed beast, fierce, petulant, and destructive; but who regards his children with not ever failing tenderness. So do we acclaim Red Samaël, the overlord of very rich and famous persons, the begetter of turbulent sons even such as is each one of us."

Here were not sentiments of which, as a vice-president of the Humane Society, and as a vestryman, and as the part owner of a tourist home recommended by the American Automobile Association, Diego could approve. But Diego did not feel that, as the citizen of a democracy in which complete freedom of speech is guaranteed to every person so long as he does not discuss anybody except white Protestants, Diego had any least call to be interfering. So Diego went forward, tacitly, along with Misroch, into the palace.

They came into a high hall paneled with ebony. It displayed twenty-seven arches with scarlet curtains hung before each one of them. Above, were nine balconies and three galleries without pillars. Still higher up, you perceived twenty-seven windows with rounded tops, all which windows were open, or else had no glass in them.

In the midst of this hall Diego observed a circular basin upon the red rim of which squatted twelve frogs, about twenty-seven inches high, carved of red stone. Every one of these frogs sat fronting the basin's center, and from the mouth of each frog spouted water, so that these twelve jets fell, in bright thin ellipses, upon the four turtles, carved of gray stone, which from the center of this fountain faced north and east and south and west. In the water which filled this gray-lined, red-rimmed basin Diego saw, moving indolently, a number of rather large crimson and gold-colored fish.

Well, and this fountain reminded Diego of the fountain in front of the main entrance to the Ponce de León Hotel, except that he now observed with disapproval, at the exact middle of the red-rimmed pool before him, and standing erect among the four gray turtles, a red stone image, far taller than Diego, which represented a member of the human male body. Diego disapproved of this image because it was depicted as uncircumcised. He reflected that this was not in accord with modern sanitary customs; and that it thus set a bad example such as the owners of the Ponce de León Hotel almost certainly would never have allowed to be displayed in their courtyard.

Yet furthermore, at the farther end of the vast high hall, upon a red-covered daïs, Diego saw a couch of carved teakwood inset with rubies, if they indeed, so Diego meditated, because of his moderate-mindedness, were not merely bits of colored glass; and this couch stood underneath a canopy of dark red satin, or again, it might be just rayon, looped up with ropes of what were imitation pearls perhaps, about the size of an alligator's eggs.

Upon this couch, and clothed vividly in scarlet, reclined a long-legged youngster whose equal for beauty Diego had never beheld. The boy's hair was red and curling; his cheeks were ruddy; and his blue-gray eyes had in them a roving and bedazzling brilliance.

In this way, and at the same instant that Misroch tactfully turned incandescent-looking from head to toes, and so vanished like a burned-out electric light bulb, did Diego de Arredondo Dodd come to his immortal father, Red Samaël the Seducer; and in silence Diego displayed the queer green stone.

## 21 ც෧

WELL, and after that, the young devil looked at the magic stone without showing any at all suitable excitement, and he looked at Diego likewise, with a ruminative air of wonder.

An over-hasty observer might have thought the

immortal boy had found something not quite desirable, or even a tinge of the depressing, in the appearance of his sedate middle-aged son. But Diego committed no such error. Diego knew that, for a man of forty, his person was still handsome enough. And besides that, Diego's second-best dark blue suit (when you wore it along with a white shirt and a black bow tie) really did make Diego seem almost exactly as if he had on a Tuxedo; and in fact, was very distinguished-looking, as Diego now reflected, with an untroubled conscience, under the devil's inspection.

"You do not wholly resemble," the youngster said, by-and-by, "the run of your turbulent and lofty-hearted, heroic brothers."

"I shall say only that I hope not indeed, sir," Diego replied. "For nobody has enough self-control to discuss his immediate relatives without saying more than he ought to."

"Nevertheless," Red Samaël continued, "it is all in the night's work, what sort of children one may happen to beget. So hail to you, my pot-bellied and middle-aged, so commonplace-looking, dear son! and do you now tell me what name you bear upon earth."

"I am called, sir, Diego de Arredondo Dodd."

"And whatever upon earth do you desire of me?"

Diego answered that he did not desire anything

in particular; that he wished merely to pay his filial respects; but that at the same time, sir, rather than appear unappreciative of your generosity, Diego could not very well be so uncivil as not to ask for a slight miracle-working such as Diego went on to describe deferentially. —Although only of course, Diego added, if it was wholly convenient, and not any least trouble.

Red Samaël had listened indulgently. But the look which was now upon his immortal young face showed a conviction that every one of his earlier dealings with imbecility had been upon a minor scale.

"—For never," said the fiend, reflectively, "during my not inextensive paternal career have I been asked for any such trumpery with which to defy time and chance, and to advance the turbulence of my children. It is my custom to bestow upon my children wealth and learning and power and seraglios and empires and yet other fine gifts of that nature."

"Your generosity, sir, is proverbial," Diego replied; "yet a proverb does not prove anything except prejudice. So you must permit me to remain sceptical as to whether, in a moderate-sized tourist home, either an empire or a seraglio could be accommodated without rousing comment."

The fiend went on, half vexedly, "Now I shall

144

have to give you whatever you ask for, of course, because ever since your brother Cain asked for the city of Enoch, it has been with me a fixed custom, my dear Daniel, to humor every one of my children."

"The name, sir, is Diego."

"Why, but yes, to be sure. You will understand, I trust, that as the centuries slip by, one's family does rather tend to accumulate. So my children have got beyond the point where I can keep quite as closely in touch with every one of them as I could desire. But as I was saying, my dear David—"

"The name, sir, if only you will overlook my persistence in retaining it, is still Diego."

"Beyond doubt it is; and I apologize. Yet why, Diego, upon this joyous occasion do you continue to regard me with disapproval? and for what reason, even while your glib mouth is speaking with a resolute civility, do your heavy eyebrows scowl?"

Diego answered: "My eyebrows scowl because they have become thick and shaggy; whereas the eyebrows of my young father are dark and slender arches. Yet furthermore, my eyebrows bristle above eyes in which, as I have noticed time and again, I mean, when I was shaving, sir, or brushing what remains nowadays of my hair, one finds contentment and acquiescence and no particular curiosity

145

about anything. But in your glittering, blue, burning eyes gleam restiveness and defiance."

"You must remember, my son, that because of Jehovah's short temper, and His old-fashioned lack of any least sophistication, I was condemned, without being given any choice in the matter, to remain eternally youthful."

"Yet that, sir, by correct social standards, and I mean of course without taking up any of its theological aspects such as a communicant might just as well, and in fact far better, consign to oblivion, and C.O.D. at that, appears beside the mark. That is not a sound excuse. It seems hardly an extenuation for a father's being so very much younger than his son, or indeed at all younger than his son. Not even in St. Augustine, where for the benefit of the tourist trade we maintain a Fountain of Youth, is any such behavior customary; nor, as you must permit me to tell you, would it fail to evoke criticism in any other part of Florida, even in the more dissipated circles of Palm Beach or of Miami."

"Yes, but, my son, it so happens we are not in Florida—"

"Let us not dwell upon that, sir; for what do you conceive must be my emotions when I am compelled by circumstances to concede that, through no fault of mine, my own father is a fiend in Hell!"

The fiend answered: "Even so, you cannot be

*146*

more deeply horrified than am I, to behold in one of my own sons an epitome of the middle-class virtues. Since time began, the children of Samaël have been proud and daring and rebellious; they have been conquerors; they have submitted to no authority; they have followed after their own desires without any faltering. Whereas you—! Why, but it troubles me to consider your oily and smug, long-winded respectability, you Diego de Arredondo Dodd! for you might have been begotten by Oriphiel or Michael or any other time-serving archangel between his hosannas. However, let us have a look at your record."

The fiend was now sitting erect upon his teakwood couch; and now, just somehow, in his lap lay a large volume bound in red morocco. He consulted its pages; and his young face saddened.

"My child," he said reproachfully, "but this will never do! You have stolen money, as well as six umbrellas and a cigarette case; you have forged two checks; you have perjured yourself upon various occasions, eleven times before a notary public, and twice upon the witness stand; you have been the cause of five innocent young girls' needing to palm themselves off deceivingly in matrimony as an unopened package; and you have helped fourteen married women to commit adultery."

"Nevertheless, sir—" said Diego.

"For nine widows, and in a forbidden locality," said Red Samaël, "you have revived the ardors of a honeymoon; you have begotten four illegitimate children; you have killed three men; you have made incorrect income tax returns; and furthermore, you have evaded the Selective Service Act, as well as jury duty."

"Even so, sir," Diego protested, "every one of these deplorable events occurred a fair while ago. And if only you will permit me to explain about them—"

"But that," Diego's father continued, "that appears to be a complete catalogue of your misdoings. I blush to regard this so slender list of ragamuffin performances. It quite fails, as you must let me tell you frankly, my unfortunate misguided son, to maintain the traditions of our family. You ought to have been over-riding human and divine laws with some trace of distinction."

"I can see your point of view, sir, which, most naturally, is that of a fiend in active practice," Diego granted. "And I in turn blush to admit that even these offences were youthful errors into which I strayed, without any creative touch of premeditation, when I was an inexperienced boy; and for every one of which I have repented long and long ago now that I am middle-aged and have reformed."

"Even so, my son," the devil returned, consolingly, "it is never too late to relapse. And as concerns this so foolish bit of trumpery for which you have asked—"

"Well, but then, sir, you see," Diego pointed out, with mild obstinacy, "wishes are like wives, in that we come by them without ever knowing just how. And besides, this is something I did not ever attain. Pretty much everything else which I wanted, or at least thought that I wanted, in the time of my slapdash early manhood—a time upon which, as you must let me confess, sir, I now look with the high-minded abhorrence proper to a clergyman or to the plaintiff's lawyer in a breach of promise suit—I did manage to get. At any rate, I got everything which I wanted, more or less, so to speak, and found the market price was excessive—"

"That," said the devil, "is an economic rule in all pleasure-seeking."

"—Except only," said Diego, "this one desire. And I am afraid, sir," Diego added, piously, "that it would be a sad comedown for your reputation, to have it reported that a son of Red Samaël had failed to obtain any one of his desires. So without consulting my own wishes, either one way or the other, it now appears my plain duty to you for me

*149*

to be gratifying my desire. And it is not right for anybody to neglect his duty."

"Yes, but—" said Diego's puzzled young father, just as all young persons have always needed to say when they considered the axioms of their elders.

Afterward the fiend shrugged; and Red Samaël said, half sulkily:

"Oh, very well, then. Thout, tout a tout, throughout and about, rentum tormentum!"

## 22 ෴

IN THIS WAY did Diego enter into that castle which when he was young he had imagined to be the appointed home of Catherine Mary Zapo and Diego de Arredondo Dodd.

He came first into the rotunda which occupied the great central space of the main building; and now facing him were eleven broad marble steps which ascended to the dining hall. To his right and to his left, large corridors loomed vaguely; and through them moved heroic persons. The pavement under Diego's feet he observed to be a mosaic, composed of tiny bits of white marble, adorned with twenty-four circles of some grayish-green stone, of which he did not know the name. From above and around Diego, the rotunda was illuminated by a host of lions' heads, each one of which held gingerly, between its teeth, an electric light bulb.

The immense dome under which Diego stood was supported by eight pillars of quartered oak, carved with four caryatides standing back to back at each pillar; and the rotunda was four stories in height, forming as it ascended, at each story, incredible arcades and tall galleries, of which the arches and the columns were all of a different design.

Moreover, here to express the matter at its very mildest, the interior walls and the ceiling of this dome were painted. They were painted with swans and lyres and stags' heads and rams' heads; with mermaids and arrows and globes and swords; as well as with dolphins and seashells and torches and salamanders; and with peacocks and cornucopias and snails and a number of butterflies also.

These minor objects, however, were but a part of the background for eight glowing, huge, and noticeably well-fed-looking symbolic figures. For now, some sixty-odd feet above Diego's head, sat ponderously Adventure in full armor, and Discovery in blue robes, and Conquest in red ones, and Civilization in a white nightgown, engrossed by the contents of what appeared to be a large scrapbook; and now above Diego stood Air and Earth and Fire and Water, for whom the painter had failed to provide any chairs.

Yet higher up, as a sort of pictorial postscript, were some cupids and eagles and shining helmets and the riggings of one or two ships.

Diego, in brief, now found himself to have entered a place which, except that everything was rather more spacious and even more brightly colored, seemed remarkably like the lobby of the Ponce de León Hotel.

He wondered about this resemblance. Then he reflected that when this place was imagined, the florid and so liberally ornamented Spanish Renaissance architecture which was invented for the special gracing of St. Augustine by Messieurs Carrère and Hastings, and such mural paintings as during the 1880's were allowed to be perpetrated by George W. Maynard, with the connivance of H. T. Schladermundt, had represented the utmost which a long-dead boy knew about magnificence; so that quite naturally this boy had followed after the cluttered expensiveness and the flamboyance of the Ponce de León Hotel when Diego de Arredondo Dodd designed his dream castle.

But the people whom a time-revised Diego now found in its corridors were not at all like those tourists who, as Diego's mother used to phrase it, had more money than was good for them. Instead,

Diego went among persons about whom very long ago a boy had read lovingly, and with whom he had populated his dream castle. And some of them Diego could recognize, but a number of them had gone out of his memory; and to Diego that seemed a sad thing, because once upon a time he had been intimate with all these noble and heroic beings; and now he had not anything in common with them.

Nor would it ever be possible, he knew, for him to be reading the poems and romances and the obsolete high-hearted novels from out of which these people had been mustered without feeling that the qualities which these people exhibited were traits unknown to mankind; and so had to be shrugged aside as being merely the futile inventions of irresponsible and minor fiction-mongers who did not meet with the requirements set by the judges of either one of your book clubs.

For Diego, I must mention here, in the event of my not having told you about it earlier, was a member of two book clubs. He thus kept in touch with all the very best modern literature; and so, whenever he attended a dinner party or a reception, and every cultured person among the guests who were present at it, started to discuss the best-selling novels, then Diego was spared the humiliation of having to confess sadly,—

"I am sorry; but I never got around to reading that."

—Which was naturally a large comfort to Diego, and made secure his social position.

Well, and at the clerk's desk Diego found upon duty a proud porter who was dressed in the way that people used to dress in King Arthur's times in your book called the *Mabinogion*. Only, it was not your book any longer; and you did not know what had become of it, or of the boy who had once loved that book, and who had borrowed from it this porter.

## 23 ❧

DIEGO NOTICED, to begin with, that this porter wore a coat and a surcoat of flame-colored satin. About his neck was a broad band of gold lace; and on his feet were high shoes of variegated leather, which were fastened by golden clasps in the form of pelicans that were each thrusting its beak into its own breast, so Diego found out later.

The name in raised letters upon the rectangular bronze sign which stood on the proud porter's desk was Huandaw. And when Diego asked to whom this castle belonged, the astonishment of this Huandaw appeared so limitless that he came out from behind his desk into the lobby. It was then that Diego first saw the porter's shoes.

"Now, by the hand of my friend, fair sir," spoke Huandaw, "but thou art at the court of young Diego de Arredondo Dodd—"

"So I had inferred; and the fact is, to a certain extent, gratifying—"

"—And if thou holdest not thy peace, small will be thy welcome. That," the porter explained, with an indulgent shrug, "is what the youngster created me to say to everybody. For in these parts everything within the reach of imagination belongs to young Diego de Arredondo Dodd, inasmuch as his imagination created everything around us, as well as you and me."

"That his imagination created you, proud porter, I do not deny. But I am certain—and for some reason or another reason it seems a reflection fraught with moral solemnity—that no helter-skelter young Diego de Arredondo Dodd could have been able to imagine me."

"Indeed, fair sir, you are not one of his more happily inspired efforts in the arena of creative art; yet even good Homer sometimes nods, as the saying goes."

"Come now, Huandaw, but that was not at all my meaning; and a proud porter who quotes Horace smacks of anachronism."

"That is because our creator, fair sir, was never at pains to imagine me thoroughly. I am but a minor detail to his dream castle. The place needed a retinue of proud porters to make his dream complete. And so I was sketched in, lightly, along with my fellows in office—who are Gogicwc and Llaeskenym and, upon Saturday afternoon and all public holidays, Pennpingyon. Thus casually, thus imponderably, was I created by the imagination of young Diego de Arredondo Dodd, without his ever bothering to give me any traits in particular."

"Why, but yes, I quite comprehend your sad predicament," said Diego. "You are like Rosencrantz in *Hamlet*, or J. Donald Duck in the weekly comic page of the *New York Times*' Book Review, or Millard Fillmore in history. And I wonder if you do not find it unfair for you, like them, to have been created, without having any choice in the matter, thus trite and trivial, or, as we scholars phrase it, thus wishy-washy?"

"You have raised a point, fair sir," the porter replied, reasonably, "as to which I cannot well speak with conviction. For I have never been anything else except only just such gaudy and threadbare stuff as their dreams are made on, customarily, by almost all youngsters."

"And so, Huandaw, with a continuing defiance

*156*

of likelihood, you have been reading, not merely Horace, but Shakespeare also!"

"Ah, but you must remember," was the proud porter's self-defence, "that I exist only when young Diego de Arredondo Dodd happens to think about the entrance to his dream castle upon a Monday or a Thursday. Between whiles, one has to fill in the time somehow."

"Yes, but," said Diego, instructively, "if you need to kill time, now that war work and the higher emotions of patriotism have gone out, and the radio programs have become to the intelligence of their hearers a rather too direct affront, then you ought to be joining one or another of the book clubs which appeal to the finer instincts of every member of one's family, just as I did after my literary likings also had reformed and settled down."

"Should I indeed, fair sir?"

"Beyond doubt, Huandaw; for any one of these book clubs will supply you every month with a book weighing not less than three pounds, and at a reduction from the publishers' price, to be read with pleasure; to be discussed with delight; and to be retained in your home library with pride."

"I admit, fair sir, that I am not a member of any book club—"

"That is obvious," Diego answered, sadly, "because if you did not continue to miss so many new books which you know you will deeply enjoy, then you would not be concerning yourself with Shakespeare, no, nor Horace either. You instead would be employed, far more vitally, for the rest of this month, by concentrating your mind upon the month's masterpiece by Francis X. Flubberdub."

"But," said the porter, "but I do not think that even the most learned persons in these parts have knowledge of Francis X. Flubberdub."

"Why, then, Huandaw, the atmosphere of the castle of young Diego de Arredondo Dodd is not abreast with advanced cultural values," Diego went on, at his most informative. "For the novels of Mr. Flubberdub are warm and earthy. They appear to have been written with an acetylene torch upon asbestos. His books are full of pungent phrases and hair-trigger action, which is forceful, uproarious, and inimitable, because it is shot through with flashes of brilliance and has been woven into a rich, colorful tapestry that has the feel of a classic. One might even go so far as to assert that as a literary colossus, in trousers, at any rate, Mr. Flubberdub has but one living equal upon the horizon this month."

"Yet if, just for one moment——" said the porter.

Diego said: "I allude, of course, to the powerful, apt, and charming prose of Gideon Gibberish, which has pulled no punches in a novel of unleashed passion written with a relentless vitality and drive. His current book is an outstanding, red-blooded miracle of first-class art. It is nostalgic, hilarious, bawdy, heart-warming, and head and shoulders above the run of fiction that has been on the bookstalls in a dog's age, or at any rate, this month."

"Now, by my faith—" said the porter.

"I admit, however," said Diego, "that such merely masculine qualities do not satisfy all connoisseurs of the higher reaches of the month's reading-matter; and so, upon sound literary grounds, a ripsnorting new novel by Natalie Babu English has but lately gone into its eleventh printing, in the very same instant that a million and a half delighted readers are acclaiming the ever-living fame of Laura Caconym Nugatory for the rest of this month."

"I think," said Huandaw, "should you permit the observation, fair sir, or any other observation—"

Then Diego said: "—Which is as it should be. For either one of these ladies is the biggest money's worth of your life. They are breezy, refreshing, rather shocking and indubitably worth while. In her latest novel Miss Natalie Babu English has written a world topnotcher. It is an achievement of the very highest æsthetic rank, and it will combine nicely with a hammock, a cool drink and a

warm afternoon, if only because it is a deeply moving and thoughtful book without its equal anywhere among the most lively satirical writing
which I have read about in the *New York Herald
Tribune* this month."

"You speak with conviction," said the porter,
"and yet, if only you would permit anybody else
to be speaking—"

"—Whereas," Diego replied, firmly, "Miss Laura
Caconym Nugatory has just published a love story
which you will never forget, with a surge to it like
the surge of the sea. Her current novel will grip
you and appeal to your imagination. It is the most
powerful and absorbing and magnificent job in
fiction which the five judges of one of my two book
clubs have ever read during the last six weeks. It is
a novel with the compelling rhythm of a swing
band. It is debonair, delicious, unique and concrete.
I feel it my plain duty, however," Diego added,
conscientiously, "to tell you in advance that you
may find it well-nigh impossible to lay down this
book, because it narrates a story of tremendous
impact."

"I thank you for that warning, fair sir—" the
porter began, yet again.

"And I should perhaps condole with you," Diego
went on, "as to the circumstance that your deficient inventor, young Diego de Arredondo Dodd,

did not have any chance to study the methods of those creative artists who now adorn an unequaled literary epoch of monthly immortality. For then —my poor, unrealized, vague Huandaw—you might have resembled one or another more forceful character in the tons and the freightcar loads of masterworks which are produced every month by Francis X. Flubberdub and Gideon Gibberish and Natalie Babu English and Laura Caconym Nugatory; and with which both of my book clubs enable their members to kill time and discrimination. You also, Huandaw, might have been absorbing and breezy and concrete and earthy and unleashed. Your existence might have combined the surge of the sea with a relentless vitality and hammocks and hair-trigger action and acetylene torches and moving picture rights. But one cannot have everything; and the notions of this young Diego de Arredondo Dodd were his own notions in a day which will not ever again be reviving."

"No doubt, fair sir, such was the way of it," said Huandaw, in the middle of a polite attempt to make yawning masquerade as a hiccough; "and in any event, this is the way to his apartments."

With that, just somehow, Diego found himself to be looking at the appearance and into the thinking of a boy who once upon a time had left St. Augustine in order to become very rich and very famous, and so as to see something of the world at large; and in the same room was young Catherine Mary Zapo.

## 24 &

THEY WERE strangely beautiful dear youngsters; and as Diego looked at them, with an odd commingling of pride and of compassion, his eyes were not unblurred, because he knew that time would be changing these children, by-and-by, into sedate and well-thought-of and well-balanced persons such as are the mainstay of our civilization. And Diego knew likewise that this changing was proper and desirable, and for the true benefit of everybody concerned; yet it seemed wasteful, somehow.

It followed that when Diego said, "All hail, your majesties!" his voice was not wholly steady.

Now to tell you what happened after that, is difficult. To set down in full the colloquy between the boy that Diego had been and the middle-aged person whom Diego had become is tempting. It would be pleasant to record, for your improvement, all that eloquence which was displayed, by both participants, when this young Diego, like the ghosts in the Huguenot Cemetery, considered that Diego de Arredondo Dodd had fallen short of what was expected of him; and to tell also about the superior and complacent wisdom with which middle-aged Diego tucked his thumbs under his armpits and replied conclusively at full length. A complete account of their talk, with no word of it omitted, would be moving and salutary; and it would embody a fine apologue.

So I can but regret that when the middle-aged Diego said, "All hail, your majesties!" then a thing happened which he found to be troubling; and this thing was that neither young Catherine Mary nor young Diego de Arredondo Dodd looked up toward him, nor did they seem to hear his speaking.

"And so," said the proud porter, pensively, "you were right, after all, when you denied that he imagined your existence. You had not any perceptible part in the life which young Diego de Arredondo Dodd foreplanned for himself, that is evident."

"No," said Diego; and then he cried out, with unhappiness,—

"But, Huandaw, they do not observe you either!"

"She does not ever observe anybody except Diego de Arredondo Dodd," the porter returned, "because that is how he imagined all women would always be forever."

Diego shrugged as devil-may-carishly as he could manage. But he thought it better not to argue this point.

*163*

"—And he does not observe me when I am here, in these apartments," the porter added, "because I exist only when young Diego de Arredondo Dodd happens to think about the entrance to his castle upon a Monday or a Thursday, and imagines me to be at the room clerk's desk."

Then Diego said, still speaking without joyousness, at random,—

"That appears to me to be nonsense."

"Most naturally, fair sir," said Huandaw; "for the dreams of young men, and all which they imagine, are nonsense. Moreover, you are real; and young men are blind to realities."

"Yes," said Diego, and he gulped a little, "it is I who am real! And the proud boy who sits before me heart-deep in dreams does not any longer exist in reality! and to the reality of our hand-to-mouth living here upon earth he was blind until after time and conformity, and some hard knocks also, had become his oculists."

Then Diego stayed silent. And his moderate-mindedness was troubled, now that he regarded a dream which had once been his, and the absurd vainglory of this dream which, for one reason and another, he did not find laughable, now that the dream of a boy had been revived. For, as I have told you, Diego was looking both at the appearance of and into the thinking of this boy, now that young

Diego de Arredondo Dodd sat at ease in the royal suite of his castle; and, at this instant, was glancing over the morning mail. . . .

## 25 ࡳ

WELL, and in the morning mail which you were glancing over, there was a letter from President Calvin Coolidge, and a letter from Pope Pius the Eleventh, and a letter from Governor Al Smith, and a letter from John Drew, and a letter from the lately deposed Kaiser Wilhelm, with a Dutch stamp on it, and a letter from H. L. Mencken and George Jean Nathan (which was signed by both of them), and a letter from Clarence Darrow, and a letter from the Prince of Wales, and a letter from Jack Dempsey, and a letter from John D. Rockefeller, and a letter from Al Capone, and a letter from Rudolph Valentino.

For the glory of your name and your power and your wisdom had spread over land and sea; so that every one of these great people wanted to get your consent to, or your advice about, the most important possible doings.

Your seneschal was keeping the letters which had come to you from just oodles of ladies. He would deliver them to you later, in private; and you would read them in the bathroom, so that

Catherine Mary would not be getting upset about these ladies' letters.

It was not that Catherine Mary had any real reason to be jealous of any woman, because your eyes and your heart and your thinking were filled with the beauty of Catherine Mary, and with the wonder of her dearness to you, so that, excepting only yourself of course, you thought about and you cared for nothing else in comparison with Catherine Mary.

Still, Catherine Mary was sort of high-tempered sometimes. She did not like the way in which all those other women kept on falling in love with you and trying to get you to sin splendidly, or at any rate, to give them just one hour of happiness which they could remember always.

That was why you had arranged, tactfully, when she was out having five o'clock tea with Queen Mary, for your seneschal to put aside the letters which they wrote to you every day. And after you read these letters, then every day you tore them up, and you put the pieces of them in the seat, and you flushed it out very carefully, so that Catherine Mary would not know anything about these letters and be getting upset.

While you were glancing over the morning mail, Catherine Mary waited for you to get through with it; and she was reading too, in the book which she always read when you were busy and could not talk to her about yourself and what you thought as to things in general. She did not ever want to read anything else, although every one of the very best new books lay upon the table at her left hand.

You could see *Jennifer Lorn* in the semblance of a half-morocco binding; and *The Tattooed Countess* in a maroon binding; and *Balisand* in sage green; and a dark blue copy of the Fourth Series of *Prejudices;* and there were a whole lot of other books of which you approved benignantly, because they were meant for the small civilized minority, and offended the *boobus Americanus*.

But Catherine Mary had laid open among, and on top of, these less interesting volumes a very thick red-covered book, that had red-mottled edges to the pages of it, which was too heavy for her to be holding in her lap with comfort. She was reading over and yet over again, because she did not ever care to be reading anything else, in this copy of *Who's Who in America*, those two and one-half solid columns, so very much longer than any other article in it, which told people about the life and the travels and the doings, and the honorary degrees from the colleges, of Diego de Arredondo Dodd, and about the clubs and the societies he belonged to.

So you and Catherine Mary were well enough content now that Diego de Arredondo Dodd had become very rich, and very famous, and had seen

*167*

something of the world at large. You had seen
enough of it, at any rate, to make certain that in
all the world your like had not ever been heard of
before; and now, in your dream castle, you lived
among the most splendid and heroic associates
whom anybody could imagine. But you outrivaled
every one of them, so that they did homage to you.

And you remembered always to be gracious
upon every occasion of this nature. When Mr. Coolidge, or Achilles, or d'Artagnan, or the Prince of
Wales, or Joseph Hergesheimer, or Sherlock
Holmes, or John D. Rockefeller, or Sir Launcelot of
the Lake, or anybody else of that sort, did homage
to you, then you thanked them at once; and you
said it certainly was nice of them.

It was kind of curious that you did not ever get
stuck up about it, but went right on being real
polite to everybody, just as if Diego de Arredondo
Dodd were not more wonderful, and richer, and
more famous, and a heap smarter, and more
splendid, than everybody else all put together. . . .

## 26 &

"Now but upon my word," said middle-aged Diego,
when he had gone thus far in young Diego's thinking, "it does not seem plausible that I could ever
have been like that. And yet I was like that when

I was young, and had fire in me, and a self-confidence in me which did not know any limits—along with a sort of fineness in me, too, you unfortunate, foredoomed, self-centered, prancing, ignorant, smug, young, rampageous jackass, drat you!"

Still, it was a large blessing, and it was a marvel also, that this boy had developed into a well-thought-of citizen. He had blundered into some imbroglios, and even into a few technical misdemeanors, during the process of his development, Diego granted. Yes: but then how very easily, well, upon perhaps eight occasions, this boy might have blundered, instead, into a penitentiary—or for that matter, when you came quite seriously to think about one or two of those technical misdemeanors, into the customary hearty breakfast which would have preceded his release from imprisonment through the aid of an electric chair. You simply could not ever tell how a jury may feel about anything, inasmuch as the main desire of every juryman is just to get back to his own business.

So one ought to be satisfied. And in fact one was wholly grateful that this visionary youngster had traveled toward Diego's complete respectability through no more ugly mishaps than a bare handful of indiscretions which stayed undetected, and for which one could repent in private, without there being any need for an Elk and a treasurer of the

Laymen's League to be shocking his fraternal and business associates with the knowledge that at any time these mishaps had occurred.

"Thus all ends happily enough," Diego decided. "We inhabit an imperfect world, so all philosophers tell us; and I am a part of it."

And then, just as when Diego had confronted the ghosts in the Huguenot Cemetery, he bowed low before his former self, half jeeringly, he hoped, and yet too, he was certain, with a sort of heartsick desperation.

"—For the moral of your majesty's ending," said Diego, "would seem to be that in every law, as in every lady, good luck may find a loophole."

He shrugged afterward; and with that comprehensive gesture, Diego walked out of the castle which the dreams of his youth had builded, and with which Diego had no longer any vital concern.

So did he come out of his dream castle into a paved courtyard which was divided into twelve sections. Now to the right hand and to the left of him, the gray pavement under Diego's feet was inscribed mystically with large triangles; and it was marked also with three numbers, which were repeated over and yet over again. These numbers were ten and eight and seven, each one of them being colored, as was likewise each one of the twenty-four triangles, black.

Here was, in brief, a paving which surprised Diego, because he recognized it at once. For he was now walking, he perceived, across the shuffleboard court which lies south of the city of St. Augustine's fine Spanish Mission Style Recreational Center and Tourist Club.

In this way did Diego de Arredondo Dodd come back out of the sunset, and away from the dreams of his youth, across twelve shuffleboard alleys, into the adjoining Huguenot Cemetery.

There were no ghosts to be seen in this quiet graveyard now, as Diego noted with relief; but Diego was perceptibly remote from being alone now that he confronted yet another person with whom, as in the case of Herbert Darnell, he had not expected to have any further dealings.

*Part Five* &

# WHICH GETS A GOODLY HERITAGE

*"How shall I put thee among the children, and give thee a pleasant land, a goodly heritage of the hosts of the nations?"*

—JEREMIAH, III, 19

## 27 ह~

"And so, my child," said Red Samaël, smiling, "so I now find you, of your own accord, leaving your dream castle."

"And you find me likewise," Diego replied courteously, "more grateful than I can say for your kindness in enabling me to enter this castle."

"Yet you have not chosen, I infer, to become its permanent tenant."

"With the complete frankness, sir, which ought always to exist between father and son," said Diego, at his most amenous, "I must tell you that it did not impress me as a suitable residence for a middle-aged couple such as Catherine Mary and I have become. We would not feel at ease among its high-pitched unhumorous innocence. The boy who contrived my dream castle believed that human beings could be strong and staunch and heroic in their virtues, and in their iniquities too for that matter; so that he peopled his heart's home with such dear monsters as no middle-aged person who, to a rea-

sonable extent, I mean, sir, has seen something of
a more rational way of living can approve of, or
desire to have, as his daily associates."

"These sentiments pain me," said the devil.

"Yet with middle-age, sir," Diego explained,
"and with the acquiring of a responsible position in
society, one comes to know that any very lofty
ideals are better left to the pulpit and to political
statements, where nobody will bother to take them
seriously; and that anywhere else an heroic way of
thinking, or of approaching the criminal code
either, is apt to upset matters in general."

"Oh, but come now," said Samaël; and with that,
the fiend sat down, and he made himself comfortable, upon the broad, low, flat-topped tomb of
Charles Downing, who upon account of his having
been Always Bold and Generous to a Fault, died
Universaly regretted, upon Novr 24th, 1841—so
nearly as you could make out the last digit, which
was not clear—after having been, for several years,
a Member of the Territorial Legislature of Florida;
and who was Twice Elected to the Congress of the
United States of America.

Now to every side of Red Samaël, and the vivid
scarlet of his attire, showed a green tranquilness
varied only by the dark grays and browns of yet
other tombstones. High overhead, the boughs of ancient live oaks intermingled so as to shelter this part

of the Huguenot Cemetery with an unbroken roofing of somber, small and hard-looking leaves, of which the coloring was so obscured as to appear black rather than green. And here and there, from this high roofing, depended very long tentacles of pale Spanish moss which moved vaguely, but perceptibly, as though these tentacles were breathing.

It was a place of peace, this so wholly quiet, twilit graveyard. And it made you feel, just somehow, so Diego reflected, that not anything anywhere was really worth anybody's worrying about, inasmuch as all human matters had been settled very long ago upon a not ever to be changed but a sufficiently lenient basis.

Diego wondered, mildly, that in any surroundings thus beautiful and so sedative, his father should still be speaking in a tone of lively dissatisfaction. But then young people were like that, always. Young people seemed never to be content with affairs as affairs stood; and you found it rather a pity.

"Come now, Diego," Red Samaël repeated, "but the common-sense of your middle-age has betrayed you into talking about exalted ideals in a manner of which as an infernal spirit I cannot approve. No, not nowadays, my dear son, now that our labor troubles and our housing problems have made it a necessity for every infernal spirit to cultivate friendly relations between mankind and Jehovah;

and thus to protect our country against an invasion by damned souls. Hell's foreign policy, you conceive, now calls for romanticism and for high thinking and for an unflagging superiority to mere logic among all human beings."

"And for what reason, sir?"

"Why, but without being hoodwinked by these particular virtues," young Samaël asked, in surprise, "how could mankind forgive their Creator for having created them what they are? and then holding them to any sort of account for being futile and pernicious by nature? However, your addiction to common-sense is easily remedied; for I shall bestow upon you not merely that opulence and that earthly power such as are your birthright as a child of Red Samaël. You shall likewise have back your youth; and that will settle all; for young people know how to regard common-sense with a religious amount of contempt."

Then Diego shook his head with decision.

"I enjoyed my youth, sir. But once is quite enough, as the saying runs. And so I decline to have back my youth. It almost certainly would lead to my committing a number of legal indiscretions so awkwardly as to be detected; and for a vestry-man to do that, cannot be tolerated. Yet furthermore, the resulting scandal would be the ruin of the Bide-A-While Tourist Home."

"But—" said Red Samaël.

And he was allowed to say not one more syllable upon account of the promptness with which Diego went on talking instructively.

"If only you will stop interrupting me, sir, and if you will overlook my becoming somewhat free-spoken, because of my sincere interest in your welfare, and my natural sense of filial duty, it is the main trouble with you yourself that you are young. Now I admit that for an immortal personage, and in view of your having fallen into disfavor with Heaven, this trouble may be incurable. So I do not hold it against you, or at least not personally. You observe, sir, I am trying to be fair-minded. I say merely that your being young does not alter the fundamental principles of correct behavior."

"Still—" said the devil.

"Just to begin with, sir," said Diego, in the tone of voice which befitted a vestryman, "your persistent and perhaps chronic youthfulness extenuates your conduct with the wives of Adam, possibly, to a certain extent. But it does not by any means justify your having gone into rebellion, a while later on, against that Supreme Being Whose legal claims to omnipotence, now that He has settled down and become a Christian, are recognized by the best-thought-of people everywhere; and which in fact have been endorsed by the Protestant Episcopal

Church in the United States of America ever since the sixteenth of October 1790, so my prayer book informs me."

"Yes, but it was a good deal earlier than 1790, Diego, that because of my inability quite to hit it off with the Lord God of Sabaoth, I elected to leave Heaven—"

"I know, sir," Diego assured Red Samaël, in the more genial tone of a Kiwanian, and with that patience which we all owe to the mistakes of our parents.

Afterward Diego too sat down. He sat, as a preliminary glance informed him, upon the adjoining flat-topped tomb of Mrs. Eliza C. Whitehurst, who in all the relations of life had fulfilled her duties with fidelity, prior to facing the pangs of dissolution without any terror, upon 3rd June 1838, because her heart was without guile.

Diego was thus enabled to confront his infernal father at ease and with a friendly air of indulgence. Diego reared back expansively; and his two thumbs now went into his two armpits.

"—For six thousand years ago, or thereabouts at least, according to the *World Almanac*," Diego resumed, "you were still young, or rather, what I mean is, sir, you must have been even younger than you are today. You were inexperienced; and you were misled, it may be, by your companions.

My poor father, but I quite understand! I very well know how it is when a pack of youngsters, such as you rebelling angels were in those days, get together, and when one thing leads to another, so to speak. It is just as when I came near being involved in some rather serious trouble over poor Roger Maldahyde's having killed himself in my apartments—"

"Upon West Tenth Street," said the devil, quietly.

"I find it flattering, sir, that you should have preserved a so accurate account of my past doings in that morocco-bound red book of yours," said Diego, somewhat startled, but still speaking equably. "However, poor rash Roger's inconsiderate behavior is not to our present purpose; and my alibi was unquestionable, as the coroner's jury agreed without any dissent."

"Even so, Diego, I have noted in your record that if only this jury had been somewhat more thoroughly informed as to what became of the money he had with him—"

"Well, yes, I know, sir. I admit that, to a certain extent at least, they did not know everything. But then who does know everything? Besides, sir, I am referring to the legal aspects of an affair which was settled formally, a good long while ago. I believe in treating a legal decision with respect, if only because, without law, one cannot hope to have order; and the jury's verdict was suicide while of unsound mind."

Diego paused for an instant; and he smiled benevolently, from the genial suburbs of patronage, quite as though he were addressing the Young People's Service League.

"As I was saying, then, sir, when yet again you interrupted me, most boys have always been more or less apt to become obstreperous, so to speak, out of sheer playfulness and because of their high animal spirits. All that part of it is natural; and it is pardonable enough in the depressing light of human nature. And much more so, of course," Diego added, handsomely, "if through no fault of one's own, one's nature happens to be superhuman; and is thus made, I daresay, at least twice as difficult to get along with quietly. So I can well understand, sir, how you came to be evicted from the hierarchy of Heaven and from the official responsibilities of a seraph—"

"Your approval heartens me, Diego; and if only you would consent to stop talking for one half-second—"

"But I am not approving, sir; or at any rate, I am not approving of, but to the contrary, I am reprehending without hesitation, and in the strongest possible terms, your later wild ways. I find it my plain duty to rebuke the persistent levity which

*182*

has led you into so many centuries of amorous pursuits and of seductions and of adulteries among the women of all known nations; and which has made of my own father's name a synonym for lewd and illegal conduct. To anybody with a proper amount of filial feeling any such behavior is necessarily distressing. Perhaps I might express myself somewhat more exactly by saying that it appears to be unnecessarily distressing. The English language, sir, as you may have noted, is at times as double-faced as its makers. Not for one moment, however, would I deny that such indiscretions may have their pleasant side, even though I do not pretend to speak in the light of personal experience—"

"In fact, five girls and nine widows and fourteen married women," said Red Samaël, in a condoning manner of which Diego could not approve, "amount to but little less than celibacy."

"But no, sir, I would not say that, or at least, not in public. After one has reached forty, you see, it sounds far better to disapprove of any and all such affairs with a suitable amount of violence. For this reason, I have repented about each one of those twenty-eight injudicious darlings separately; and I have forgiven the way in which the dear creatures led me on. If ever you come to be my age, sir, you will know that, like illogic and fine needle work, seduction is a feminine accomplishment.

*183*

That is why these sad irregularities have to be expected in the life of each and every inexperienced boy. But it is not right, sir, for anybody to keep on being misled forever by flibberty-gibbet young women who happen to have more or less physical beauty. There is a limit to all things except only the regrets of a spinster and the dull-mindedness of a democracy; so that you likewise, my poor father, during the last few centuries or so, ought to have found time to repent and settle down."

Diego's father replied, speaking with the pensive and that partly shamefaced gravity which is peculiar to youth:

"You forget, Diego, that it is the duty of a patriot to defend the welfare of his country. And my country is Hell. It follows that, in the line of duty, I have to allow myself to be led astray by as many young women who combine good looks with a sound standing in society as I may happen to find persistent. I see to it afterward that they are detected in their sin, and their respectability is imperiled. They then regret having yielded to my improper advances. They repent heartily. They repent with no less vigor than you have repented, Diego, over one or two slight errors in your own past such as we perhaps need hardly discuss—"

"In fact, sir, as a director of the Humane Society,

I have always believed in letting sleeping dogs enjoy the full benefit of an undisturbed nap—"

"And after the affair has been hushed up, my child, in the way that a respectable family always does hush up such affairs, then my victims, like you, Diego, become self-righteous and vociferous, sturdy church members, just such as, I am certain, your dear mother was. In part, this is because after one has been embraced by Red Samaël, one finds mere flesh-and-blood lovers to be disappointing, and carnal sin loses personal zest. But above all, you misguidedly reformed Diego, it is because nothing else can so deeply stimulate an aging gentlewoman's sense of religious duty as do her fond memories of past peccadilloes which the younger generation is repeating enjoyably. My victims thus become shunned paragons of unamiable virtue; they expire in the odor of sanctity; and straightway they enter into Heaven. In this manner, my dear son, do I defend Hell"— and the complexion of the young devil heightened, diffidently—"with an always reliable weapon; and I labor nightly so as to add to the ranks of the blessed."

"Come now," Diego granted, brightening, "but an argument, like a virginity, may be lost without leaving any hard feeling. I admit seeing a new point of view as to your infamous career; and I rejoice to observe the philanthropic, or at any rate, as we scholars put it, the philogynic, aspects of what, in a manner of speaking, might be called your church work."

"I have not ever believed in being ungenerous, not even to oneself," Red Samaël replied nobly; and thus speaking, he arose from his seat upon the mortal remains of former Congressman Charles Downing.

"Meanwhile, Diego," the fiend continued, "the theme of our most pleasant chat reminds me that, at this very instant, it so happens, I have an engagement. I am certain that, as a Southern gentleman, you would not see me so deficient in gallantry as to be late in keeping an appointment with a gentlewoman in her own bedroom. And so, my child, inasmuch as you decline to wish for unlimited wealth or unlimited wisdom, and since you refuse to accept an empire or a seraglio or any other of those trinkets which my sons ordinarily request when they come to me in the prime of their youth, instead of waiting as you have done until your more moderate-minded middle-age, I am at a loss to decide what I can do for you—just at present," the fiend added, quite unaccountably.

"Well, sir," Diego admitted, so as not to appear ungracious, "it is true that at forty a small steady income seems to be enough, and one does not hanker after famousness, or an empire, or any more wisdom. And Catherine Mary, so to speak, would not at all fit in with a seraglio. Yet it is equally true that at our tourist home over yonder we really do need an oil circulator."

The fiend looked at Diego for some while; nor did the surprise of Red Samaël eclipse his disappointment as to his son's meager aspirings.

"I know, sir," said Diego; and for Diego, he spoke almost meekly. "I know that, as the son of an infernal spirit, I ought to be a great deal more high-spirited. And to me too it seems a sort of comedown, because for a long while I believed that I wanted glory and magnanimity and splendor and, well, so to speak, sir, that I wanted a castle in the sunset. But I find I do not want these matters nowadays. I really would much rather, sir, if it be just the same to you, have an oil circulator so as to take the chill off in the morning."

Red Samaël sighed. He raised both hands. And he said, so nearly as Diego, later, could recall the gist of his father's observations:

"Archima, Rabur! Bathas over Abrac! Flowing down, coming from above Aheor upon Aberer!"

—After which, the fiend remarked, "Chava-joth!" And he continued:

"The desire of your humbled and time-parched heart, my broken-spirited poor son, has been installed. It is one of the latest models, of cast-iron construction, with an all porcelain cabinet and a stainless steel burner. It has side reflector doors, a down-draft hot blast and a removable fire pot. It will heat from four to six rooms; and it ordinarily retails at $149.50. But I still think, Diego, that if only you would consent to become heroic, and famous, and wealthy—"

"So far as goes being wealthy, sir, it is quite true that once upon a time I did hope to become wealthy beyond the most gaudy and extravagant notions of a European relief program. Young men are like everybody else in that they do not understand our income tax system. If ever I got into the higher brackets, I know nowadays, I would be left miserable for life. And it follows that upon the whole I very much prefer to jog along, unharried by any more Internal Revenue agents, upon a small steady income out of the tourist trade. They are sufficiently bigoted as affairs stand, I can assure you, and almost every year at that, when it comes to taking an unsympathetic view of our business expenses and the necessary thousand and one repairs— Which reminds me, sir, that should it be within the reach of your power, and I mean, of course, without inconvenience, we ought not to forget about repainting the house, or at any rate, the front of the house. And an oil tank, so to speak, had very nearly slipped my mind."

"Turius and Shurius Inturius!" Diego's father answered sadly, with the same gesture which he had employed earlier. "A tank containing 250 gallons of fuel oil now stands to the rear of your tourist home; and the entire building has been repainted, in cream color with a red trim. But while I have the place in hand, my poor dear son, if only you would let me transform it into a palace—"

"Not with the servant problem what it is today," Diego replied stoutly. "For Catherine Mary, our having to housekeep in a palace would lead to unending trouble, because of their unreliability and their impudence. Moreover, sir, these are annoyances which a married woman takes out on her husband, in common with all other annoyances."

"And so, Diego," the depressed, great-hearted young devil asked, "now that you have repudiated your dream castle, in favor of having your place of business repainted, and a more modern heating system installed in it, you can think of no more to wish for?"

"Nothing whatever, sir, now that your generosity has provided all which I really require. I admit I had thought of asking for a sedan car, in of course the middle price class. But after all, the car which we now have is hardly six years old; and ever since we had another motor put in and some seat covers, it appears to be in excellent condition.

In fact, if only the truth were known, I believe it is a great deal more reliable than these flimsy new models which they are getting out nowadays. So there is no need for us to be wasteful."

—All which, of course, were sound considerations. Yet because of the extravagant and toplofty notions to which young people are subject, Red Samaël still could not hide utterly his grief over his son's moderate-mindedness, now that a petulant, rather dear-looking and misled, tall child was replying to the sane counsels of common-sense:

"It is you who are being wasteful, you dunderheaded, forever-talking, blundering Diego, now that all the pleasures and the glories of human life are at your disposal. And in place of them you are asking me for an oil circulator!"

"Yes, but, sir, ever since I can remember, I have wanted an oil circulator, just as I have wanted to have our tourist home repainted properly and to marry Catherine Mary."

Then the fiend said: "These things will not content you, Diego, because in spite of your thinning hair and of your responsible position in society, you must remain always a son of Red Samaël. And so before very long you will become tired of your smug, tenth-rate way of living and of your stupid, pale-eyed, large, over-masterful wife; that restlessness which is my restlessness will be reviving in your time-parched heart as a fire rekindles among gray ashes; and once more you will be desiring to become very rich and very famous."

Still smiling, the fiend touched Diego's breast.

"But above all, in your heart—which is now thumping rather faster, Diego—you will be desiring to be made young again, and to have back in you that fire which is my fire, and to be wandering about the world at large with that high-handed pleasure-seeking, and with that inconsideration of all other persons' notions, which are the heritage of every son of Samaël; and by which you also, Diego, were guided once upon a time before you reformed and dwindled into a lickspittle, into a mere limp flimsy washrag, Diego, adrip with soft soap. When this thing happens, my dear son, you will be coming back to me for your birthright; and then I shall be granting all your desires."

"That is kindly said, sir," Diego replied, a little frightened now, but still speaking with composure. "And I would not think of disputing it is wise to stay prepared against all contingencies. So I shall keep in mind your most generous offer to let me have anything in the world which I may desire, if only because, in these days of strikes almost every minute, and of a labor shortage everywhere, one really does not ever know just what, sir, may, so to speak, turn up."

"Farewell to you then, my son, for a brief while," the demon answered, with a look of quiet fore-knowledge such as Diego found to be remarkably discomforting.

With that, they shook hands; and as Diego stood there, holding the firm young hand of Samaël the Seducer in his own time-crinkled, slightly spotted hand, Diego was moved to speak concerning what seemed to him his father's over-devotion to church work and about the excess of the zeal of this fiend in helping so very many handsome young women, through the time-approved avenues of carnal sin and a proper amount of contrition for it, to become saints in glory.

Yet Diego stifled this impulse. For after all, the youth of his large-hearted and over-generous young father remained eternal; the youth of Red Samaël spurred him relentlessly toward gynecology; and nothing whatever could be done about it, upon at any rate this side of Doomsday, when it might be that Jehovah would accord to the young devil's undying amativeness the favor of annihilation.

Diego sighed a little, to think of his father's sad destiny. And in the moment that he was sighing, Red Samaël vanished in order to keep his appointment with still another young woman somewhere or other, so as to qualify her for eternal salvation through repentance.

## 28 &

"YOUTH is an affliction," Diego meditated, in the while that he passed eastward through the Huguenot Cemetery, upon his way toward San Marco Avenue and the City Gates of St. Augustine, "from which all mortal beings must suffer temporarily; and it misleads us into a large number of works of supererogation such as are reprehended, quite properly, by the Fourteenth Article of the Episcopalian faith, and such as later on call for a fair allowance of sackcloth and ashes. Yet eventually all we who are blessed by having been created human and impermanent, and no less variable in mind than in body, do get over our youth and the rampageous dreams of our youth. The folly of youth's aspirations is revealed to us; we perceive that in a workaday world they, so to speak, will not work; we are thus able to dismiss them forever; and we can settle down in comfort.

"But my dear poor young father has been punished, just for a couple of youthful indiscretions with the two wives of Adam—who quite probably led him on, inasmuch as they were both nearly two weeks old at the time—by having to remain young eternally; and to be always rampageous. He may not hope ever to reach the contentment of a middle-aged and representative and tolerably well-to-do person who has reformed and settled down.

"Yet nothing whatever can be done about it by anybody, no matter how browbeating may become the dictates of filial affection! My unfortunate young father is doomed for all time. He will have to go on ravishing every female heart with his loveliness, and with the unfailing vigor of his yet other possessions, even until the Solar System has been discontinued. Forever and forever, even until Doomsday, his imperishable beauty will deny rest to all women who look upon him, because when compared with the radiance of Red Samaël, the sun will appear no brighter than a kerosene lamp. So long as time lasts, the sweetness of the voice of Red Samaël will make the conceded masterpieces of the world's very best poets, and of the world's finest musicians also, seem a stuttering and a grunting and a braying; the smile of Red Samaël will serve as an opiate to prudence; and the touch of his roving hand will be the death warrant of any woman's continence.

"It is a large grief to me, and it is a humiliation too, to have to think about my immortal young father's past, which is of a nature such as the police department and the better families of the Nation's

Oldest City could not be asked to condone; as well as about that dissolute and unalluring future which my unfortunate, forever youthful father is condemned to spend in the bedchambers of insufficiently clothed young females, and which he will have to devote to the antics of consummated affection.

"And I feel sorry for young people everywhere upon account of the romance and the reverence and—of all conceivable inconsistencies!—the importance which a young man and a young woman do very certainly, and as I myself can remember, attribute to these unsightly gymnastics.

"In fact, the young of our species are only too apt to beget, in addition to yet other by-products, a rather low opinion of human intelligence. I regard with blushes and with a mature indignation their behavior.

"Nevertheless, the Bide-A-While Tourist Home has now been repainted properly. It is now equipped with an oil circulator to take the chill off in the morning all during the tourist season. And I still have my birthstone with which to perform any number of yet further miracles, in the event of our needing some repair work in the way of new copper plumbing, which I really ought to have thought about; or of our deciding to put in an elevator, just under the stairway; or of my electing, after all, to become an heroic and wealthy and world-famous person. So I must very carefully preserve my birth-stone against any such emergencies.

"Its hellish origin I regard with repugnance; still, I do not have to tell anybody about it; and one does not like to be wasteful."

Uplifted out of all gloom by these final reflections, Diego passed through the City Gates of St. Augustine. Beneath the 8 Inch Howitzer Gun, Armament of Fort Marion, Number xv, he found lying undisturbed his neatly folded-up shadow. He unwrapped it; and after spreading it out upon the asphalt roadway, he was at pains to smooth out a few creases which made it look slightly disheveled. The night air of St. Augustine tends to be rather damp.

Then, stooping, Diego re-attached this gray shadow to his aging but reasonably well-preserved person, in the while that Diego, still stooping, and with his rump turned carefully parallel to the City Gates, repeated backwards, between his parted legs, just as his Aunt Isabel had directed,—

"Es Nes, non Nodna, Baiodos!"

After that, no longer in a magic twilight, but at 5:20 A.M. precisely, in the light of an honest workaday dawn, Diego de Arredondo Dodd started homeward toward a resumption of his temporarily put-by common-sense way of living.

*An Epilogue* 🦢

# ENDING THE DREAMS OF
# ALL DODDS

---

"*And I said, This is my infirmity; but I will remember the years of the right hand of the most High.*"

—PSALMS, LXXVII, 10

# 29 ❧

Now as Diego walked down quiet Bay Street, in the light of dawn, he observed the unnaturally long shadows of the palm trees along the sea-wall. The shadows of the trunks of these trees, falling straight across Bay Street, divided the roadway into a commendably neat series of rectangles, all equally attenuated. They reminded you of a shuffleboard court. Nothing whatever moved in Bay Street except Diego and Diego's own prolonged shadow, to the right-hand side of him.

As you passed by the glass-enclosed porch of the Bennett Hotel you did notice, to be sure, an obscured bellboy inside this porch, seen very vaguely, like a fish in an aquarium. You noticed also his slow movements as, with an infinite leisure, he swept up the porch floor for the beginning day. Such leisure was not unlike that of a fish in an aquarium. It showed you what servants were unless you kept right behind them all the time. The boy would be going off duty at six.

There was no cloud to be seen anywhere in the sky. The sky looked as though it were made of thick blue glass, or rather, it had the blue which you found in Wedgwood pottery. The sky looked as though it would be cool and solid and unyielding if you could touch it.

To your left side, upon Anastasia Island, beyond the restive and glittering, wide surface of Matanzas Bay, an irregular long line of gaily tinted houses, each having a different brisk color, showed intermittently, inset in, and partially hidden by, a serrated and a continuous dark wall of very tall pine trees which rose far above the ridged green roofs and the red roofs of these dwarf-looking houses. They were not native pines, it occurred to Diego, The Davis Shores Development people must have imported these pines. They came from Norway perhaps.

Upon the twinkling, slightly tan-tinted waters of Matanzas Bay a number of widely scattered sea gulls bobbed up and down, and they bobbed sideways too, toward the west, drifting about at random. Among these sea gulls five white-and-black small ducks could be seen, grouped staunchly together, with an air of ignoring, and in fact of resenting, the sea gulls' helter-skelter existence.

Each one of these ducks faced south. Each one of these ducks was exactly similar in appearance to all the other four ducks. Whenever, as had happened five times now, the motion of the water turned any one of these ducks toward the west, then laboriously and precisely the duck righted itself in order that once more it might face toward the south in common with its four companions. It showed you, if at forty you needed any such teaching, that to conform with your companions was natural as well as being prudent.

Such trivial matters alone did Diego de Arredondo Dodd observe, idly and disconnectedly, as in the bright dawn he walked down Bay Street at peace with all the world, now that he had been to Hell and come back again.

But in front of the Bide-A-While Tourist Home, Diego found his foster father, Bartholomew Burton Dodd. Mr. Dodd sat upon the low sea-wall immediately across Bay Street. Mr. Dodd was regarding pensively a residence which overnight had become cream-colored, and which now had brilliant red window frames as well as a brand-new-looking red roof.

And his foster son likewise Mr. Dodd regarded pensively before remarking that you did get accustomed to it, more or less at any rate, once you had married into it. That of course if you happened to have been born an Arredondo, why, then there you were! But that still, Diego, at the same time, the other members of the vestry ought to be allowed for.

## 30 ࿃

"BECAUSE you know how people are," Mr. Dodd continued, "and how people do talk in a small place where everybody knows a great deal more than everything about everybody else."

"That, sir, is regrettably true," Diego granted, with the massive unction which he kept for moral reflections; "and I have often thought that of all known human vices this habit of talking too much—"

"So long as you do it moderately and sensibly," said Mr. Dodd, "and do not go beyond improving our premises by repainting the house, even though I personally would have said white and green, it shows a quite proper feeling. And when it comes to an oil circulator, which we have been needing ever since your poor mother used to talk about it just as if money grew on palm trees, why, not even the rector ought to complain. I noticed it of course, the very first thing, when I came downstairs. It seems to be a really first-class oil circulator, Diego, such as no clergyman could object to."

"In fact, sir, inasmuch as it is merely a matter

of making our paying guests rather more comfortable, and since I knew that green paint—"

"So I am not saying that he would," Mr. Dodd
returned. "No, not even though, if you ask me,
since he came back from the war, he is a little too
High Church in his notions. But if it ever got to
your behaving like your humpbacked Uncle
Manuel, you could not expect tourists to put up
with having the ghost of a Spanish governor's
wife in and about the place, nor could you blame
them for one moment. And besides, I do not think
that any clergyman ought to be wearing a soldier's
uniform, more than half the time, almost everywhere he goes. Nor," Mr. Dodd added, with a touch
of austerity, "does it alter the principle of your
having stayed out all night long."

"It was merely, sir," Diego replied, "that I
thought it my duty to put your mind at rest as to"
—and Diego coughed modestly—"as to the possible
result of my marrying Catherine Mary. And while
I was attending to what seemed a plain moral obligation, upon account of your unfailing kindness to
me, sir, and your great-hearted indulgence concerning the unfortunate circumstances of my own
birth, well, but one thing led to another, so to speak.
That is absolutely all there was to it. Yet I really
must say that green paint—"

"And for you to be putting the tourist home in

good condition against next season," Mr. Dodd resumed, "is wholly correct and proper, because when you come to think about it, Diego, if you keep the tourist home, then the tourist home will keep you."

"So I have heard, sir; and I can assure you it was merely at the call of duty—"

"I have noticed, Diego, that you are very much like other people, in that duty never calls upon you to do anything except something which you feel like doing and cannot find any other excuse for. It is not any reason for your interrupting me. Your mother was like that, too."

"I apologize, sir, even though I really do think that in this climate green paint does not stand up well enough, as we both ought to know, after those garage shutters—"

"And," said Mr. Dodd, "it is something I am not starting any argument about, because I believe in letting people go their own way so long as they do it moderately. But for you to be staying out for the entire night, and especially if anybody were to see you coming home, at your time of life, what with your being on the vestry, where you ought to have learned how to be more careful, is quite different."

"I shall not do it again, sir; and I can make bold to promise you that after Catherine Mary and I are married next month, she will put her foot down—"

"She will," said Mr. Dodd, with conviction.

"—And will see to it, perhaps not without eloquence," said Diego, "that so far as goes the ghost
of any Spanish governor's wife—"

"But I was not talking about ghosts, Diego. Nobody ever said one word about ghosts, except just
in passing. So you ought not to keep on interrupting people in this way when I was trying to tell
you that, on account of the Zapos' being so high
and mighty, and behaving just as if they did not
have an embezzlement right in their own family
not more than ten years ago, I am hoping you
really did find out about the baby."

"Not impossibly, sir, it may have red hair. But
otherwise—"

"Now why upon earth, Diego, should it be having red hair?" said Diego's foster father.

Mr. Dodd paused. Mr. Dodd colored up a little;
and he continued tranquilly:

"Still, any number of babies do have red hair.
And when you come to think about it, Diego, that
is really their own business and not anybody else's
business. Nor is it at all important. I believe in letting everybody go their own way, Diego, even in
diapers, so long as when you are holding them, of
course, you keep a blanket or something in your
lap."

"But otherwise," Diego resumed, patiently, "there is no need for us to be fearing that any eccentric extensions, such as one finds at both ends of a cow, sir, just for an example, may be attached to the small squalling cherub, when it decides to get born and to perpetuate the honored name of Dodd. For I must tell you I have been upon a brief visit—"

"That also is not important," said Mr. Dodd, still slightly flushed and still speaking with decision. "It does not much matter how you spent the night at almost forty-one, I am afraid, Diego, so long as people do not get to talking about it. It ought to matter, of course; and upon Sunday mornings it is right and proper for us all to be thinking about it in that special light; but in every week, Diego, there are six other mornings. No, nor does it matter what dreams you may have been having during the night time, not even though"—and here Mr. Dodd likewise coughed—"not even though your dreams may have shown a quite natural interest in your own family, such as does you credit. For everybody has dreams, Diego, just as everybody has measles; but we get over both of them by-and-by."

Diego looked at Mr. Dodd for some while. Diego recollected that, howsoever incredible it seemed to him, his white-haired, plump, placid foster father had once been young. A half-frightened, middle-aged Diego comprehended, upon a sudden, that he was now in train to become exactly such a prattling and tedious and tenth-rate, time-blighted mediocrity as was Bartholomew Burton Dodd, if Diego did not take advantage of his birthright, and return posthaste to his superb young father, who as yet remained so great-heartedly insistent upon making Diego as young as Red Samaël was young forever; and who would enable Diego to become heroic and rich and famous.

Catherine Mary also was rather unbearably tedious, Diego reflected, when she spoke with an air of complete authority as to matters about which she happened not to know anything. Catherine Mary was so provincial-minded and so dictatorial —because Diego preferred not to think about a Southern gentlewoman as being exactly pig-headed—that after Catherine Mary had once promised to love, cherish and obey Diego until death did them part, then his married life would have to be very much like that of Bartholomew Burton Dodd. Catherine Mary, as Mr. Dodd had phrased the conduct of his own wife, would be finding fault with her husband, and with everything connected with her husband, all day long and every day in the year, for—as all wives always did phrase it—his own good.

And Diego would have to put up with it, more or less indulgently, and Diego would have to give in to it, just as Mr. Dodd had done, for the rest of a commonplace and a wholly unimportant existence, if Diego did not take advantage of his birthright.

Yet it so happened that Diego was fond of his domineering, large, irrational Catherine Mary; and he was fond of his tedious, prattling old foster father. He in some sort revered the dear, simple goodness of both of these stupid persons. It was a quality to which Diego de Arredondo Dodd, as being just half consciously a glib-mouthed fraud, had no pretensions. He knew that he liked this quality. He knew that he liked also his quiet and comfortable and insignificant, but safe, manner of living as the manager of a middle-class tourist home.

Diego did not wish to relinquish these humdrum matters in order to become heroic and rich and famous. Nor very certainly, did Diego wish to have back his youth again, along with a resumption of any such technical violations of the penal code as his being made young, and having fire in him once more, might entail.

You regretted having to become middle-aged and smug and tenth-rate and unspeakably unimportant; but upon the whole you preferred to have that anticlimax end the career of a no longer rampageous-spirited Diego de Arredondo Dodd. You preferred to be as safe as the conditions of human life permitted anybody ever to be.

It followed that, dismissing these hasty reflections, Diego took out of his pocket the green stone which would get for him whatever he might desire. He knew that he desired, nowadays, not to indulge his desires. So he now threw this stone over the low sea-wall into Matanzas Bay. And when he had thus ridded himself of any possible further temptation to become an heroic and distinguished person, Diego said to his foster father:

"Wise men and angry women speak the truth. You are wholly right, sir. In youth we have our dreams. But we get over our young, foolish, callow, restless dreaming, about our capacity for heroism and for picturesque iniquity, when age touches us with, as it were, an admonishing hint of oncoming eternal quiet. And then we are well enough content to settle down into the snug insecurity of a tourist home, where everybody comes and goes continually, even its proprietors by-and-by; and where nevertheless we do manage, somehow, without—as one might phrase the affair, sir—any more vain thoughts about having a castle in the sunset, to get along in comfort for a little while longer."

"I had one once," said Mr. Dodd, with an all-comprehending tranquillity. "Only, it was a ranch out West, along with Maxine Elliot, and with Maude Adams, so nearly as I can remember."

"Even so, sir," Diego stated, and he now spoke in a vein of despondence, "it is the ignoble comfort which we derive from giving up our dreams that I most resent."

"People have every reason to be comfortable," said Mr. Dodd, stoutly, "when they have a sound roof over their heads, and are getting a fair to average income out of the tourist trade."

"You are pleased, sir, to speak in parables," Diego asserted. "For this ever-changing and inconsequential and this self-concededly half-deceptive tourist trade, when you look at it rationally, seems a fine apologue for our transient human way of living here upon earth, I take it."

"You may take it or you may leave it," said Mr. Dodd. "I do not know of any other choice. People have to live as other people do, Diego, and without starting any argument about it either, if they want to keep out of trouble. I mean, of course, so long as luck lets them."

"And methinks, like the Archbishop of Tyre," said Diego, shrugging, "that this controversy might, without dishonor to any party, end with these two not inconsiderable points."

EXPLICIT